"Better be nice to me, Alex, or you won't get any ice cream," Michael Casey teased.

"Oh, Casey, I'd love some. Is it chocolate?"

A slow smile stole across his face. "I bet you'd do anything for chocolate ice cream."

"And just what did you have in mind?"

"Heh, heh, heh."

"Shame on you. That's the dirtiest laugh I ever heard." He was the most outrageous, endearing, disarming man she'd ever met. "Where are your scruples?"

"I think I left them in the kitchen with the ice cream. I know. I'll give you some ice cream if you give me a kiss."

"What kind of kiss? Are we talking about a big kiss or a little kiss?"

"A medium kind of kiss."

"Will there be other body parts involved in this kiss?" Alex asked, struggling to keep her voice stern. "Or just a lips' kiss?"

Casey's mouth curved in a devilish smile. "No more questions. I can see I'm going to have to take matters into my own hands." He watched her for a moment before leaning forward and claiming her mouth. His lips brushed across hers, softly, testing, enjoying her breathless expectation. No matter what she'd said before, Alex wanted to be kissed. He could see it in her eyes; he could sense it in her parted lips. And when he deepened the embrace, he could hear it in her soft moan of pleasure. . . .

WHAT ARE *LOVESWEPT* ROMANCES?

They are stories of true romance and touching emotion. We believe those two very important ingredients are constants in our highly sensual and very believable stories in the *LOVESWEPT* line. Our goal is to give you, the reader, stories of consistently high quality that may sometimes make you laugh, sometimes make you cry, but are always fresh and creative and contain many delightful surprises within their pages.

Most romance fans read an enormous number of books. Those they truly love, they keep. Others may be traded with friends and soon forgotten. We hope that each *LOVESWEPT* romance will be a treasure—a "keeper." We will always try to publish

LOVE STORIES YOU'LL NEVER FORGET
BY AUTHORS YOU'LL ALWAYS REMEMBER

The Editors

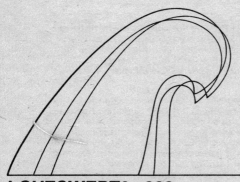

LOVESWEPT® • 303

Janet Evanovich
Manhunt

BANTAM BOOKS
TORONTO • NEW YORK • LONDON • SYDNEY • AUCKLAND

MANHUNT

A Bantam Book / January 1989

If you would be interested in receiving protective vinyl
covers for your Loveswept books, please write to this address
for information:

Loveswept
Bantam Books
P.O. Box 985
Hicksville, NY 11802

ISBN 0-553-21958-8

Published simultaneously in the United States and Canada

Bantam Books are published by Bantam Books, a division
of Bantam Doubleday Dell Publishing Group, Inc. Its trademark, consisting of the words "Bantam Books" and the
portrayal of a rooster, is Registered in U.S. Patent and
Trademark Office and in other countries. Marca Registrada.
Bantam Books, 666 Fifth Avenue, New York, New York 10103.

PRINTED IN THE UNITED STATES OF AMERICA

O   0 9 8 7 6 5 4 3 2 1

Prologue

If you took Alexandra Scott apart, piece by piece,
you would reach the conclusion that she was not
Miss America. She didn't have the classic pretti-
ness of a Hollywood starlet. It was the extrava-
gance of her features, her intense vitality and the
dramatic combination of all the pieces put together that made her into an arrestingly beautiful
woman. Her eyebrows were darker than her hair,
almost black, almost too heavy, with just a slight
angle. She had a straight, small nose, high cheekbones, a wide mouth that smiled easily, and large
deep blue eyes, their exotic almond shape testify-
ing to a Mongolian ancestry.

Every six weeks her thick auburn hair was cut
at an expensive New York salon. When it was
freshly styled, it framed her oval face in sweeping
waves that flowed into a lush cluster of soft curls

at the nape of her neck. But by the end of a work day, the voluminous, shining mass of hair seemed electric with energy and often contained pens, pencils, and an assortment of ineffective hair clips. It was pushed behind her ears, secured with rubber bands, and occasionally stuffed into a hat, but it was never defeated. Even her hairdresser had to admit that the more unruly the hair became, the more glorious it appeared.

Alex leaned forward, resting her elbows on the polished surface of the mahogany conference table, and hoped she wasn't making a stupid mistake. She was a junior vice president of a large corporation, too young to be in such a position of authority. Twenty-nine going on sixty-five, she thought ruefully. She loved her job, but she was tired—from too many twelve-hour days, too many deadlines, too many long commutes from the suburbs. But all that was about to change.

Her expressive hands loosely clasped, tightened as she prepared to speak. Her hair had been temporarily tucked behind her ears, drawing attention to the soft glow of lapis and gold earrings. She caught her glossy, full lower lip between perfect white teeth and briefly looked at each of the eleven people seated at the table. A sudden rush of emotion swept over her, momentarily flooding her eyes with tears before she blinked them away. She liked these people. They were her personal staff, and she'd miss them.

She'd prepared a speech, but it seemed inadequate, now. When she finally spoke she found herself stammering. "I . . . I know this is very sudden, but I'm going to be leaving the firm." She made a dismissive gesture over the notes lying in front of her. "I was going to make a speech about my future and our past, but it seems too impersonal. And I don't think I could get through it without blubbering!"

She uncrossed her long, slim legs clad in sheer black stockings and stood at her seat. "I've got some presents," she said, moving around the table, distributing small boxes, hugging each person. Then she smoothed her black linen skirt, straightened the matching suit jacket over her azure raw silk shirt, and turned toward the door on elegant black snakeskin slingbacks. "I don't have time to stay and talk," she said, biting her lip to keep her composure. "I have so many things to do, but I promise to write everyone a long letter as soon as I can."

She walked with the hurried briskness of a Wall Street executive, as if the faster she walked, the sooner she'd be free from the troubling, sentimental feelings that had brought tears to her eyes in the conference room. She'd done something rash and frightening, and she didn't want to dwell on it. She was, by nature, a positive person, and her positive personality made short shrift of purposeless retrospection.

She quickly traveled the long carpeted corridor to her office, all the while going through a mental checklist. All necessary forms had been completed. All projects were tidy. She marched straight to the plate-glass window behind her desk and saluted the Statue of Liberty in the harbor below. From her thirty-third floor office the monument looked like a little green toy. She held her breath for a moment, sorting through her emotions, feeling an enormous sense of relief. She felt taller. Younger. Older. Definitely excited. "Good-bye, Statue of Liberty," Alex said.

She turned from the window and pulled a pair of running shoes from the bottom drawer of the huge, elaborately carved cherry wood desk. "Good-bye, desk. Good-bye, slingbacks," she said, kicking the black shoes halfway across the room. She laced up the running shoes, slung a canvas tote bag over her shoulder and let loose a war whoop that rocked the halls of the staid brokerage firm. Once she had composed herself, she closed her office door with a smart click and walked to the bank of elevators.

"Bruno and I are going to Alaska," she explained to an elevator filled with strangers. "I've bought a hardware store."

One

Michael Casey strolled along the Juneau water-front, enjoying the briny smell of the early morn-ing mist and the screeching "*Keee*" of seabirds overhead. He rubbed his thumb across the dark stubble of beard on his chin, ruffled his unkempt sandy-colored hair and admitted that he was a bum at heart. In an hour his cargo plane would be loaded with salmon, and he would be off to San Francisco, but for now, he was at leisure to do as he pleased.

He watched the Alaskan state ferry dock and swing its boarding ramps into place. Cars and campers began to trickle from the lower deck, and a few passengers hustled down the gang-plank to stretch their legs while the ship went through the loading and unloading process. A young woman struggled along the ramp, dragging a mountain of a dog behind her. She was tall, maybe five feet eight, Casey guessed, and had the big bones and slim angular beauty of a high-paid fashion model. She paused for a second to push a mass of glossy red-brown hair behind her ears and to push the sleeves of her cream-colored fuzzy sweater above her elbows. Casey smiled unconsciously as he watched her, wondering about her destination, enjoying the spectacle she was creating as she tried to drag her belligerent dog down the gangplank.

Alex didn't notice the man watching her from the dock. She had more pressing places to direct her energy. Bruno was being a pain. She impatiently shoved her hair away from her flushed face, took a firm grip on his leash, and silently cursed her grandfather for willing her a rottweiler. Why couldn't she have inherited a small, polite animal? A hamster, or a guppie, or a hermit crab.

"Listen up, Bruno," Alex said, gritting her teeth, "I've dragged you all the way from the cargo deck so we could take a walk while the boat is being loaded, and I'm not going to give up now. Either you haul yourself down that ramp, or I'll cancel your subscription to *Dog World*." In all honesty, she couldn't blame him for throwing a temper tantrum. She'd carted the animal three thousand miles across the country in a two-seated sports car, and for the past four days he'd been kept in a kennel cage below deck.

The big black dog, obviously not impressed with

the threat, settled in an uncooperative heap at her feet.

Alex narrowed her eyes and reached for the gold-chained Gucci purse slung over her shoulder. "Okay, I guess I'll have to use my secret weapon." She took a foil-wrapped package from her handbag and waved it under Bruno's nose. "A doughnut!"

The dog's ear pricked up. His eyes opened wide.

Alex unwrapped the chocolate-covered doughnut, and Bruno heaved himself to his feet. He swayed side to side for a minute contemplating the treat his mistress held high above his head, his stump of a tail wagging vigorously, his tongue lolling at the side of his mouth in slobbering anticipation.

Alex smiled in smug satisfaction at her cleverness. "Be a good doggie and follow me down the ramp, and we'll have a picnic."

"Woof," Bruno said, planting two massive front paws on Alex's chest as he lunged for the doughnut, knocking her against the guardrail. The doughnut sailed off into space, and without a moment's hesitation Bruno jumped the rail in pursuit. He vaulted seven feet straight out, then dropped like a stone into the narrow space between the ship and the wooden slip. He hit the water with a loud splash and instantly sank below the surface.

Alex clung to the railing unable to move, unable to feel anything but a numb astonishment. The air had disappeared from her lungs, and her stomach felt oddly suspended in space. Suddenly the dog's black head reappeared, and he paddled around in confusion, searching for land and finding none. Alex could hear the labored breathing of the overweight animal. She closed her eyes for a split second, trying to pull herself together. "Dear Lord," she whispered, "someone help him." She frantically looked around, but no one seemed to be moving toward Bruno. He was going to drown in the oil-slicked water.

Michael Casey couldn't believe his eyes. That crazy broad just deep-sixed her dog! She sent him sailing off to fetch The Big One. He saw the rottweiler bob to the surface next to the ship, and from the corner of his eye caught a flash of bare thigh as the woman hiked her skirt up and straddled the railing. "Oh, man," Casey said, "what is she doing now?" She was going to jump in after the dog! He broke into a run, reaching the dock's edge just as she went under. He kicked his boots off, uttered an expletive and plunged in after her.

Alex gasped for air as she floundered in the freezing water, and knew she was in deep trouble. This water was *cold*. She was going to be a popsicle in twenty seconds, and her wet clothes felt as if they weighed four hundred pounds. She was going to die, no doubt about it. And she'd never get to wear her new raspberry cashmere sweater. A hundred and twenty dollars it cost, and she hadn't even worn it once.

A life preserver was forcefully thrust into her

chest. "Paddle this to the ladder at the end of the slip," a masculine voice shouted in her ear.

"My dog . . ."

"I'll take care of your dog!"

Alex turned to face him, squinting into the sun just in time to see another life preserver drop out of the sky. There was a sickening thud as it hit her rescuer square in the face. He went slack beside her, and a dark red slick appeared on the surface of the water as blood poured from his smashed nose. Alex clawed at his shirt, pulling him toward her, dragging him partially over the preserver. She clenched her chattering teeth and kicked out with rubbery legs, praying she could make it to the ladder. There was a splash behind her, and strong hands roughly pushed her forward.

A familiar black head looked over the wood pilings, and Bruno woofed a wet greeting as Alex was pulled from the water. Thank goodness he was safe, she thought as a blanket was draped around her and a cup of steaming coffee was thrust into her hands. She struggled to catch a glimpse of the bleeding man being helped onto the dock but was thwarted by ferry representatives trying to get her warm. She heard the wailing siren of an ambulance somewhere in the distance, and then the warning blast of the ferry getting ready to depart.

Her car was on that ferry! She grabbed Bruno's soggy leash and was swept along in a throng of people anxious to embark. She glanced back at the blanketed figure being given first aid and debated whether or not to go on. She didn't want to leave him. She needed to thank him, and there was something else, something intangible. She wanted to know more about him. She hadn't actually been able to see what he looked like, but she thought he must be nice looking. His voice had sounded sexy, deep and slightly raspy.

There was a hand at her elbow, propelling her forward, steering her toward the boarding ramp. She tried to explain that she needed to stay with the injured man, but she found the freezing water had temporarily robbed her of her voice and her ability to function forcefully.

An hour later she sat on her bunk, feeling much better after a hot shower, and allowed her thoughts to return to the man who had tried to rescue her. It seemed callous that she'd gotten on the ship and left him behind. She hadn't thanked him. She didn't even know his name. Though he'd regained consciousness when they hauled him out of the water, which gave her some peace of mind, she still felt uneasy. Not a good beginning, she decided. She hoped it wasn't a forerunner of things to come.

She turned to her map of Alaska, hoping to take her mind off the incident. They'd be disembarking in Haines shortly. The town was nothing more than a small dot on the large map, but it was very important to her. It was where she'd pick up the Alaskan highway and reach Fairbanks, she hoped, in two days. A thrill of excitement coursed along her spine as she traced the route with her finger and wondered about the cabin and hardware store she'd bought, sight unseen, from Harry Kowalski.

Two days later, Alex parked her candied apple-red BMW sports car on the shoulder of a deserted two-lane road. She made a hopeless attempt to tame her tangled hair and checked her directions. This was it. The gravel road up ahead should lead to Harry's cabin. Her stomach fluttered in a momentary rush of self-doubt. She'd never done anything this impulsive before. For many years her life had been tightly ordered, controlled by thoroughly thought-out decisions. As an executive, she'd been meticulous with details, researching all possibilities before making a commitment. It was all those damned perfect decisions that had finally done her in, she decided. She'd gone on cerebral overload, and somewhere along the line had switched from rational thought to gut feeling. One day she had awakened to a pounding headache and the overwhelming certainty that she needed to get away.

That was the day she met Harry Kowalski, and he suggested the trade. A hardware store and a cabin in the woods sounded heaven sent. Her lawyer had advised against it. No one in her right mind would quit her job and trade her home for two pieces of unseen real estate in Alaska, he had told her.

Alex gently fondled Bruno's silky black ear. "He

was right, of course," she told the dog. "But he didn't understand that I *had* to do this. The job, my condo, the closet filled with business suits and silk shirts—none of that mattered to me anymore. I didn't care if I was making a shrewd business investment. I just knew it was time to leave. I suppose I was afraid that if I gave this too much thought, I'd get cold feet."

Looking at it from her present perspective, she wondered if her gut feelings had been ill-founded. Maybe she shouldn't have trusted an old sourdough like Harry Kowalski. Prettiest little place ever, he'd told her. Nice quiet neighborhood too. And she wouldn't have to worry about traffic.

"He was right about the traffic," Alex said to Bruno. "We're the only ones on this road." For all she knew, she and Bruno might be the only ones left on the planet. She squinted through her dusty windshield at the scrubby woods on either side of the car. "Where are the shopping centers? Where are the doughnut shops and convenience stores? Where are all the people?" She draped a comforting arm around the rottweiler and chewed on her bottom lip. "I don't want to alarm you, Bruno, but this is a little more secluded than I'd expected."

Bruno rested his head on her shoulder and snuffled.

"Hey, don't worry about it," Alex said, "there's probably a pizza place hidden behind the trees somewhere. I bet we just passed fast-food burgers and didn't even know it. This is Alaska. They probably try to keep it looking rustic."

Alex shifted her car into first and attacked the narrow drive that curved steadily uphill, away from the two-lane macadamized roadway. At thirty-five miles an hour the BMW raised a dust cloud that could be seen for miles. Horrified voles scurried to remove themselves from its path, hawks and jays took to the air, and the rottweiler cowered in its seat as the sports car rattled over the dirt and gravel surface.

After the third hairpin curve Alex slowed to barely creeping and watched the odometer. When it had measured off exactly two miles she pulled the low-slung car onto the shoulder and cut the engine. A twelve-foot wide swath had been carved into the woods to her left, allowing an assortment of bushes and new saplings to grow in profusion alongside it. The twin ruts of 4x4 truck tires were the only indication that this was a traveled roadway.

Alex groaned and thunked her head against the steering wheel. "Don't tell me! This is my drive-way!" She looked around. There were no other possibilities. Wonderful. She took a deep breath and got out stiff-legged from the car, Bruno tumbling out after her. "Well, what do you think, Bruno? Should we follow this . . . driveway?" She stomped into the high grass and wished she could leave a trail of bread crumbs like Hansel and Gretel. Unfortunately, she didn't have any bread crumbs. Even if she did, she thought ruefully, Bruno would most likely eat them before they hit the ground.

Fifteen minutes later Alex struggled to catch her breath as she emerged from the woods into a large clearing. The parcel was almost perfectly square, the borders clearly delineated by stands of white birch and rugged fir. Alex felt her heart catch in her throat as she stared awestruck at the panorama surrounding her. The slope of the land provided her with a broad, spectacular view of the valley. Muskeg stretched for several miles in front of her, its monotony broken by a few small ponds that sparkled in the waning sunlight. Beyond, the snowcapped Alaska Range rose pale and serene on the horizon. She owned seven acres and a right-of-way, but she felt as if she'd just bought the world. There was no visible indication of civilization—not a road, not a curl of smoke, not a neighboring house or power line.

She inhaled the pungent woodsy air, tilted her head toward the azure sky curving above her, and smiled bravely. "Boy, this is great, isn't it, Bruno? This is the last frontier. Good-bye smog. Adios, rush-hour traffic. Au revoir, pooper scooper. Look at that sky. Smell that air."

She lowered her head and glanced around. The smile lost a little of its bravery. "Look at that . . . house." It was a log cabin, stained dark brown by time and neglect, perched atop the highest point of her property. It had a tin roof and shuttered windows. Wild roses had grown over the cabin giving it a fairy-tale quality. It looked like a troll's house, Alex decided. The idea struck her as so preposterous and, at the same time, so apt that she laughed out loud at the possibility.

Casey stalked into the clearing and stopped dead

still. It was her! Her and her big, dumb dog. What the devil was *she* doing here? A protective reflex action brought his hand to his nose. He tenderly touched the Band-Aid and grimaced. Take it easy, Casey, he told himself. This is just some bizarre coincidence. Maybe she came to say thank-you. No, she would have come up to the house. He watched her take a quick survey of the land and then focus her attention on the cabin. She shook her head, and her low husky laugh carried over to him, making his toes curl in his shoes and a stab of heat flash through his groin. Well, don't just stand there with your mouth hanging open, he muttered to himself. Say something!

"If old Harry caught you laughing at his house like that, he'd feed you piecemeal to the raccoons."

Alex whirled around. She'd been so engrossed with the landscape that she hadn't heard the man approach. He had a knife stuck into his belt and a gun slung halfway down his leg. In her mind that placed him alongside New York street gangs and lunatics escaped from Rahway prison. For the first time in her life she felt genuinely threatened. A lump of fear rose to her throat when she realized he was standing between her and her car.

Casey grinned and shook his head, his eyes openly appraising the woman in front of him. She was a knockout. A little bedraggled, but lean and classy in her designer jeans and forest-green silk shirt. She looked like a woman who was used to exercising authority, and he considered readjusting his opinion of her as a dingbat. There was intelligence behind those blue eyes and a grim determination to the set of her mouth. He was sure she had no idea who he was, and that her initial reaction to his sudden appearance had been fear, though that had quickly changed to something else. Something mysterious. "You look like a woman who's just been cornered by a grizzly."

Not a grizzly, she decided. Grizzlies were big and shaggy with beady eyes. This guy was a ten. He wore a navy flannel shirt that had obviously been through many washings, but looked tailor-made to fit broad shoulders that tapered to a flat stomach and trim waist. The sleeves had been rolled to the elbow, displaying strong tanned forearms lightly covered with blond hair. He was narrow-hipped and lean-legged, and his faded jeans clung to his body in such a way that the hard muscles of his thighs and his obviously well-endowed masculinity were subtly displayed. His sandy-colored hair was partially sun-bleached and in need of a cutting. When he smiled, his hazel eyes were enhanced by laugh lines that testified to an outdoor life and a healthy sense of humor. A fresh scar slanted across his straight boy-next-door nose and angled across his left cheekbone. A Band-Aid stretched across the bridge of his nose, partially hiding a multicolored bruise. The impression of ferocity produced by the scar was counterbalanced by a generous, sensuous mouth that curved at the corners. For a brief moment Alex smiled while she imagined him as a little boy. He would have been completely unmanageable and mischievous and totally irresistible. And he wasn't so different now, she decided, reaching the conclusion that his smile was probably more lethal than his gun.

Alex held her hand up. "Stop. Don't come one step closer, or I'll sic my dog on you."

Bruno looked at Casey and wagged his tail. The animal stepped over to him, sat on his booted foot and smiled hello.

"You mean this ferocious beast?"

"He's very protective."

"Yeah. I can see that."

Alex narrowed her eyes. He was laughing at her. What nerve. She felt like punching him in the nose, but obviously someone had beaten her to it. And what was he doing on her property anyway? She should have him arrested for trespassing. "So who are you? And what are you doing here?"

"Michael Casey, and whoever you are, you're on private property. You drove that flashy car on *my* private road, scaring the daylights out of half the wildlife on this mountain. Now if you don't mind, I'd like you to take your big dumb dog and haul your cute little tush out of here."

Harry had told her about Michael Casey. He was her only neighbor, and he was supposed to be old. My good old friend, Casey, Harry had said. And so here was old Casey, insulting her dog and ordering her around. She placed her hands on her hips in furious indignation. "My dog is not dumb. Whoever I am is Alexandra Scott, and I'm going to leave my cute little tush here for as long as I like.

This is my land and my cabin and that pathetic excuse for a driveway is mine too!"

"That's impossible. Harry Kowalski owns this patch of land."

"Harry Kowalski sold it. He moved to New Jersey to live with his daughter, and I bought this land from him."

"Oh, swell. You probably own swampland in Florida too."

"Something wrong with this property?"

"It's a beautiful piece of land, but it's a little . . . primitive."

"Actually, I was led to believe that it had a few more improvements," Alex said, casting a furtive glance at the driveway.

"Harry hasn't lived here for over three years. He moved into town when he broke his hip. The place has gotten kind of overgrown."

"Well, Bruno and I will just have to whip it back into shape. Won't we, Bruno?"

Bruno sat motionless on Casey's foot. He blinked in the fading sun and yawned.

"Boy, this dog can really handle excitement," Casey said, scratching Bruno's ear. "How old is he?"

"I think he's pretty old. He was my grandfather's dog. When my grandfather died last year, Bruno came to live with me."

"You should put him on a diet. He must weigh two hundred pounds. My foot is falling asleep."

"I wasn't home very much. He didn't get enough

exercise." She made a sweeping gesture with her hand. "Harry said all the cleared land is mine."

"Yup."

Alex pointed to the cabin. "And that cabin. Is that the only cabin on the property?"

"Yup."

"Oh, boy."

Casey felt a sinking sensation in the pit of his stomach. "You weren't planning on living here, were you?"

"Yup."

"Oh, boy," he echoed, his eyebrows rising slightly. Harry Kowalski was an old scoundrel. He'd sent this woman on a five-thousand-mile wild-goose chase, knowing perfectly well that she'd never be able to live in the crude house. He almost felt sorry for her, but there was something about Alexandra Scott that discouraged pity. She seemed invincible.

"It looks . . . cute," Alex said hopefully.

"It's well built and still sturdy. So far as I know the roof doesn't leak. Those are the high points. After that it's pretty much downhill."

Alex thought of the hundred and fifty-five thousand dollar Princeton condo she'd just left and rolled her eyes. She'd blithely traded a Jacuzzi for an outhouse, and the astonishing thing was that she felt no remorse over it. She'd been a victim of burnout. And then she'd had her biological clock to contend with. She'd found it increasingly depressing to pass by the baby-food section in the supermarket and know there wasn't a baby in her immediate future.

A sad smile tipped the corners of her mouth. She had to admit, this had been just a tad too drastic. If her mother ever found out about this, she'd have her committed. The smile grew wider at the thought of her mother's reaction to a house without cable TV. Yes, indeed, her mother would definitely think she was crazy. But her mother would be wrong. Despite the problems with her newly acquired property, Alex felt fairly sane and satisfied. She was simply walking to the beat of a different drummer, she told herself. Besides, she'd always rallied to a challenge, and this certainly was a challenge. "Okay, Bruno and Michael Casey, let's go take a look at this wonderful cabin."

Two

Casey and Bruno grinned at each other and trailed behind Alex. They followed her into the little cabin and squinted in the darkness. It was almost square, consisting of one large room with a sleeping loft built into the back wall. Remnants of a mattress lay strewn across the loft and spilled onto the floor below. An ominous black iron cookstove, bordered on either side by dusty shelves, dominated the wall to her left. An ugly, crude plank table sat forlorn in the center of the room, illuminated by the weak light barely filtering through the grimy windows.

Alex felt her heart sink. Never in a million years had she expected anything like this. It was a hundred times worse on the inside than it was on the outside. Not even a troll could live in this squalor. "Yuk," Alex said. "Did Harry actually live here?"

"For twenty-two years. There are lots of cabins like this stuck away in the woods."

"The Alaskan way of life?"

"For some."

With the heel of her hand, Alex wiped a circle of dirt off a window and stared with delighted surprise at the scarlet sun setting behind the valley. "That's incredible," she said breathily.

Casey's gaze dropped from her elegant shoulders to her perfect backside. "Incredible," he agreed. He reluctantly raised his eyes and walked to her side. "There's a moose that strolls across the muskeg every morning. If you look out this window around ten A.M. you'll see her just about dead ahead. And in the winter, when the ground is covered with snow, the whole world will sparkle red and pink and orange as the sun rises above the Alaskan Range."

Alex continued to watch the sunset. She'd lived her entire life staring at dumpsters, parking lots and privacy fences—and now she had her own moose to look at. "I think I'm going to like Alaska," she said. "Where's the nearest supermarket?"

"The nearest store is Bud's Grocery, and it's about eight miles down the road," Casey said, enjoying the faint outline of a lacy bra beneath Alex's silk shirt. "This shirt is pretty," he told her, his eyes following the path of his hand as he trailed it over her shoulder and down her arm to her elbow. The silk was cool and slick against his palm; the woman was warm and firm. She'd be nice to hold close, he thought. Nice to kiss. Nice to . . . He realized she was shivering. "Are you cold?"

Alex was cold and hot at the same time. The dampness of the dark cabin had penetrated her thin shirt, but Casey's touch was sending a surge of heat through her. There was something about the way his mouth turned up at the corners that made her want to clean his house, make his meals and tuck him safely into bed each night, and there was something about the way he filled out his jeans that made her want to crawl in next to him. He was, without a shadow of a doubt, the most attractive man she'd ever seen. If he didn't take his hand from her, she was sure the soles of her sneakers would melt.

She took a step back and wrapped her arms around herself, partially out of embarrassment and partially to protect herself. "I fell off the pier a couple days ago, and the water was so cold that I'm still having trouble getting warm. Chronic hypothermia." She smiled weakly. She was babbling. She hadn't been this flustered since sixth grade when she lost the top to her bathing suit in the surf at Point Pleasant.

Casey ran his hand through his hair. She wouldn't have been in the water so long if she hadn't had to rescue him. Now she was probably going to catch something—a cold or pneumonia. And he'd be the one who'd have to take care of her because he was her only neighbor. She'd probably expect him to make her soup and wait on her hand and foot. He gritted his teeth at the rush of pleasure that thought brought him. Casey, he told himself, your thoughts are traveling in dangerous directions. He unbuttoned his flannel shirt and tugged it from his jeans. "Now that you're in Alaska, you have to dress more sensibly," he said, helping Alex into the shirt, carefully buttoning each button and rolling the sleeves to above her wrist.

Alex stood absolutely still, barely breathing, while the warmth of his touch radiated from her heart to her fingertips. It was like being microwaved, she thought, silently admiring the broad expanse of masculine chest hidden under a green T-shirt. Casey-Barstow, Inc., Air Cargo was printed in large white letters across the shirt. "Are you Casey-Barstow?"

"I'm half of it."

"Are you rich?"

"Yup."

Alex sighed. It didn't seem fair to have been given a body like that and to be rich too. He must have been right at the head of the line when God was giving out stuff.

Casey looked at his watch. "In another half hour it'll be dark. My house is about an eighth of a mile up the hill. You can stay with me tonight, and tomorrow—"

"Are you crazy? I hardly know you."

Casey grinned. "I'm offering you the use of my house, not my body."

"Oh, hah!"

"Oh, hah? What does that mean?"

"It means I don't trust you. For Pete's sake, you're wearing a gun."

"It's in case I run into a bear."

"How awful! You mean you'd shoot the poor defenseless creature?"

Casey stared at her, nonplussed. "You ever see a bear?"

"Of course. Lots of times. In pictures. On television. Once in a zoo."

"You ever see a bear up close? Really close?"

Alex pressed her lips together in annoyance. "Not lately."

They glared at each other for a moment. Casey shifted his weight and an enigmatic smile twitched at the corners of his mouth. "Would you trust me if I wasn't wearing a gun?"

"Absolutely not." Harry had given him a glowing recommendation, but Harry was an old man. Harry didn't have to worry so much about hormones.

"So, you think I'm more dangerous than a bear?"

He was clearly laughing at her again. How insufferable. "I suppose your overblown male ego enjoys that ranking."

"Puts me at the top of the heap of local predators lusting after your voluptuous body. Probably not a bad assessment."

Alex looked him straight in the eye. "You're lusting after my voluptuous body?"

"Nothing to worry about. I can control my lust, if you can."

"Oh, great."

His smile deepened into a triumphant smirk. "Got the hots for my body, huh, toots?"

"It's a pretty nice body," Alex conceded.

Casey took her left hand and examined it. "No ring. Can't be married. Engaged? Living with someone?"

"Nope."

"Sworn off men?"

"Heavens no!" Alex snuggled inside the borrowed shirt. It was still warm from Casey and smelled wonderfully male, like camp fire and pine and a hint of musky after-shave. "One of the reasons I came to Alaska was to find a husband."

"Oh, boy." Just what he didn't need. Old Harry did this on purpose, his idea of a joke. That son of a bear was probably laughing his fool head off in New Jersey.

"You don't have to look so alarmed. You're not my type," Alex told him.

"What's wrong with me?"

"You're much too handsome. And you're rich. I want someone plain. Someone a little boring."

Casey didn't want to marry her either, but he didn't like being rejected. "I refuse to give up my money, but I could try to be boring."

"I don't think so."

"Why do you want someone boring?"

"Not exactly boring, more like stable. Someone with roots. Someone with common sense. Someone who's good at being contented. Someone with plain brown hair."

"Someone who has all the qualities you lack?"

"Yeah. How did you know that?"

"You're obviously as crazy as a coot." Casey pushed her out of the dark cabin. "So where are you staying tonight? Are you going to sleep in the cabin? With the mice and the spiders?"

Alex made a face at him. "No, I'm going to sleep in my tent. I'm all prepared. Before I left New Jersey, I bought nine hundred dollars worth of camping equipment."

"Have you ever used any of it?"

"Nope."

"Have you ever been camping before?"

"Nope."

"Do you at least know how to set up this brand new tent?"

That was another reason she wouldn't consider marrying Casey—he was a chauvinist, and his superior attitude was raising her hackles. "I'm sure it comes with directions," she said defensively.

"Uh-huh. Let's go get it and see how good you are at following directions."

An hour later Alex stared at the bright orange and blue tent spread out on the grass, looking like a giant toadstool. "I could have done that."

Casey wiped a trickle of sweat from his hairline. "Yeah. I could tell by the way you kept asking if it was upside down. I hate to rain on your parade, but I don't think you're going to last three days without a hair dryer." What he really believed was that she was beautiful with or without a hair dryer, and if he hadn't been there to help, she would have had the tent up in half the time.

Alex opened her eyes wide and wrinkled her nose in outrage. She closed her mouth with a snap when she realized she didn't now what to say. She'd been thinking the very same thing. She'd expected something rustic when she made the deal with Harry. Something that involved a fireplace, blue enamel mugs, braided rugs. It never occurred to her that she'd have to do without a hair dryer. She tried unsuccessfully to slick down her wild mass of windblown tangles. How was she ever going to land a husband without a hair dryer? She pressed her lips together. The sort of husband she wanted wouldn't care about her hair. He would see beyond that. Everything would be fine, she assured herself. She stuck her chin out. "Hmmmph."

"Hmmmph? I just insulted your ability to cope with life on the last frontier, and all you can say is hmmmph?"

Alex sighed. "You got me on the hair dryer, but hey, you have to be flexible about these things. You have to be brave and resourceful." She smiled at him. "Anyway, this can't be nearly as tough as trying to find a parking place in Manhattan."

Casey chuckled. "Yup. This is going to be a piece of cake for a tough cookie like you." He fluffed her sleeping bag while she stood watching helplessly. He chucked the bag and her backpack into the tent and zipped the front flap. "Don't worry," he said gently. "You bought a good tent. If you keep it zipped shut, you shouldn't be bothered by mosquitoes or critters. And if you don't eat peanut-butter crackers in your tent, you won't have to worry about the bears and raccoons." He pointed to the trees. "If you look through the trees, up toward the top of the hill, you can see part of a building. That's my house. I'll leave the door unlocked. If you get frightened—"

"I won't get frightened."

"Uh-huh." He stood with one hand at his hip, looking down at her. The line of his mouth tightened. "Dammit, I don't like leaving you alone down here."

"I'm not alone. I have Bruno."

"Bruno is about a thousand years old. He's obese, and he has a foot fetish."

Instead of responding, Alex unzipped the tent opening, went in, and sat down cross-legged on her sleeping bag. Wondering if Casey was serious about the bears and raccoons, she opened her mouth to ask and then decided against it. If he'd been teasing her, she would feel stupid. And if he wasn't teasing her . . . maybe it was best not to know.

Casey peered in at her through the screened window. He didn't want to leave. What was it about this woman that kept dragging him into dangerous waters? He felt a ridiculous compulsion to protect her, when it was painfully obvious she didn't need any protecting. Go home, he told himself, never come back, and she'll take her search for a husband elsewhere. He cleared his throat and stuffed his hands in his pockets. "Well, good night."

"Good night." Alex watched him walk toward the tree line. When he disappeared into the woods, she waited, listening for his footsteps to fade. In a short time a golden light appeared through the trees at the top of the mountain. He was home. And he had electricity, the rat.

Alex concentrated on the blackness that surrounded her. It has a velvet texture, a thickness that was almost tangible. There wasn't so much as a sliver of moon in the sky. Nothing stirred in the forest. The birds had long ago finished singing their night songs. There was no hum from a refrigerator, no drone of cars. She gazed out the screened window at the wooded mountain and shivered in the cold Alaskan night. She might have given her heart to Alaska, she thought, but her body still belonged in New Jersey. She zipped the window shut, removed her shoes and slithered fully clothed into her sleeping bag. She lay rigid, listening to the eerie stillness of the wilderness, and contemplated Casey's offer. He was up there in his house right now, all snug in a soft, comfortable bed. One without rocks under it. "He probably even has a pillow," she said. "Why didn't I think to bring a pillow? I can't sleep without a pillow."

She shifted uncomfortably and closed her eyes, but the vision of Michael Casey refused to be erased. She was sort of stuck on him, she admitted. Who wouldn't be? The man was gorgeous. And he was funny and sweet at the same time. Too bad he was all wrong for her. The man oozed excitement. And besides, he shot bears. "Yeeeess," she said with an involuntary shiver.

An owl hooted in the woods behind her. "Hear that, Bruno? That's an owl. Boy, it really is neat being in the woods, isn't it?" She tried to read her watch, but it was just a blur in the blackness of the night. Stars hovered over the small tent, illuminating the earth only enough to differentiate trees from sky. "No flashlight," she murmured. "I bought nine hundred dollars worth of camping junk and didn't think to get a flashlight." She had lost track of time; she didn't know if she'd been lying there for hours or minutes. She huddled deeper into her sleeping bag, trying to avoid the cold that clung to her face. "How can anyone sleep like this?" she practically shouted. "I'm a sprawler. I can't sleep in this dumb thing."

Bruno opened one eye. The skin on his forehead wrinkled in what might have been construed as anxiety. The anxiety passed quickly, and the eyelid drooped closed.

Alex sighed. "Things will be much better in the morning. Tomorrow we'll get to work on the cabin. And tomorrow we can go in to College and see the store."

A stick cracked not far off, and there was a scuffling in the underbrush. Every muscle in Alex's body tensed. Her breathing slowed as she listened. Bears? Her heart skipped a beat. There was more noise. This time it was definitely closer to the tent. This was it! she thought. There was an animal out there, a bear or a rabid raccoon. She remembered nightmares she'd had as a child. Monsters chased after her to tear her apart limb by limb, and she couldn't run away because her legs were paralyzed. She would open her mouth to scream, but no sound would emerge. It was like in the dream, she thought wildly. It was coming to get her, it was going to be terrible.

Her teeth chattered uncontrollably. She should do something! But what? She narrowed her eyes at Bruno, sound asleep in the middle of the tent. If she pitched him out, the bear would eat him, and then wouldn't be hungry enough to eat her. She was immediately seized with guilt. How could she even consider such a thing? He was grandfather's dog, for goodness sakes! Her friend and protector. Alex gulped air and tried to calm herself. Open the tent flap, she ordered. Maybe it wasn't a bear, maybe it was something small and cuddly.

The tent shuddered as a large form brushed against the front flap, and Alex felt a scream lodge painfully in her throat.

The zipper slid down and Casey peeked in. "I couldn't sleep," he said. "I kept worrying that you'd go off looking for an outhouse and never be seen again." He set down a large flashlight and tossed a pillow in her direction. He stepped in and zipped the tent shut behind him. "You look kind of pale. Are you feeling okay?"

"I feel fine. Bruno and I have been having a good time here."

"Not afraid?"

"Not me. Bruno was a little worried for a while there, but I calmed him down."

"Yeah. I can see Bruno's just a bundle of nerves." Casey grabbed the dog by the legs and attempted to haul him across the tent floor. "Damn, I can barely budge this beast. What the devil have you been feeding him?"

"Everything. The dog is a compulsive eater."

Casey finally rolled Bruno into a corner and threw a sleeping bag on the floor beside Alex.

"What are you doing?" Alex asked, cringing at the hint of hysteria in her voice.

"I'm sleeping here. I didn't think my chances were very good at getting you up to the house, so I came down here."

"I don't want you down here."

"Tough patooties."

Alex made a futile attempt to sit up in the zippered bag. "Now listen, Casey, I don't know what you had in mind, but I don't intend to share my tent with some strange man."

"I'm not strange. A little frustrated from time to time, but not strange."

Alex frantically worked at the zipper on her sleeping bag only to get it stuck in the fabric halfway down. "Dammit. If I could just get out of this, I'd pop you one in the nose."

"Yeah, I know. You're hell on noses."

"What do you mean by that?"

"Think about it."

Alex looked at him. The new scar. The bruise. The voice. "Oh, no." It seemed impossible, but it was he. She was surprised she hadn't immediately recognized the voice. She didn't think she'd ever forget that husky whisper. And she'd romanticized their meeting in her mind, assuming that she'd mystically sense the presence of the man who tried to rescue her. Now here he was, standing in front of her, and not only hadn't she recognized him, but she wasn't even sure if she trusted him.

"I suppose I should thank you for saving my life," Casey said.

"No, I should be the one thanking you. It was stupid of me to go after Bruno like that. I didn't realize the water would be so cold." She touched his Band-Aid. "I'm sorry about your nose."

"It's okay." It wasn't his nose he was worried about, he thought. It was his mind. It wasn't listening to reason. He kicked off his hiking boots and zipped himself into his bag. "I don't know why I have this insane compulsion to rescue you. Lord knows you're perfectly capable of taking care of yourself."

"Exactly. So you see, it's really not necessary for you to stay here with me."

"Wrong. I have to get up early tomorrow morning and fly to Juneau. I'll never make it if I have to spend the night worrying about you. Besides, I'm not sure my insurance covers crazy broads who get eaten by bears on my property."

Casey took the pillow and tucked it under his head. In one swift movement her reached out and grabbed her sleeping bag and pulled it to him, wrapping her in his arms. Much better, he thought. Now that she was safely beside him, he could relax. He nuzzled the brown curls resting on his shoulder and pressed his lips lightly against Alex's ear. "Go to sleep."

Go to sleep? Was he kidding? She was wrapped in the arms of a man she'd known approximately four hours, and he expected her to sleep? She made a halfhearted attempt to shift away from him.

"Stop wriggling around." he said, drawing her even closer. "Relax."

Relax, she told herself. After all, this was the man who jumped into the freezing water to save her and her dog. This was the man who put her tent together. Besides, Harry would have told her if Casey was an ax murderer or a serial rapist. Harry wouldn't have sent her up here to die. She listened to the steady beat of Casey's heart and his even breathing, and she knew he was already asleep. She squinted into the darkness in an attempt to see his face, but the only thing visible was the shiny Band-Aid.

Alex awoke slowly, struggling through drowsiness and wondering vaguely about the cool temperature of the morning air. She stretched within encircling arms and instinctively snuggled next to the warm figure beside her. What a glorious morning, she thought, tipping her nose toward stubble on a chin. Stubble? Alex opened one eye and groaned. She was sleeping with what's-his-name. "Damn!" she exclaimed, jumping to her feet, still wrapped in the confining bag. Her eyes opened wide. "Oh, no!" she swayed back and forth for a full minute trying to regain her balance before toppling head first into Casey's outstretched arms.

He propped himself on one elbow, letting Alex sprawl across his lap. "Most of the women I've slept with haven't been in such a hurry to leave my bed."

"I'm not most women."

"I've noticed that," he answered dryly.

Alex ungracefully wiggled out of the sleeping bag, feeling annoyed at the idea of other women in Casey's bed. Not that he mattered to her, but she had a strong inclination to take a hatchet to all those nameless other women. She tugged her shoes on, searched her suitcase for her Benetton sweatshirt, and looked to Casey with a hopeful expression. "Do I have a bathroom?"

"You have a hand pump next to the cabin and a clump of highbush cranberries to hide behind if you're the modest type."

"Geez."

"Are you still planning on living here?"

Alex slipped the sweatshirt over her head and stepped out into the chilly air. She took a moment to appreciate the pungent aroma of damp moss and pine and to look at the sun sitting huge and pale over the Alaska Range, coloring the sky yellow and gray and making the tiny ponds glitter. "Of course I'm going to live here. Just look at this. Boy, this is the life."

"Honey, you don't even have an outhouse."

"I'll build one."

"In a month the first snow will be falling. An average winter temperature is twenty to thirty degrees below zero." Casey waved his hand toward the cabin. "How are you going to heat that thing?"

"How did Harry heat it? I assume he used that monstrous cookstove."

"That monstrous cookstove takes wood. Lots of wood. Can you chop wood? They don't deliver logs to your doorstep up here, you know."

"Then I'll get a kerosene heater. I think I can manage to pour kerosene."

"You have no electricity. How are you going to plug in your electric rollers?"

Alex plucked a handful of hair and held it up for his inspection. "I don't use electric rollers."

"Looks like you use an electric eggbeater. Where are you going to plug in your electric eggbeater?"

"Abe Lincoln didn't have an electric eggbeater, and I don't need one either."

Casey closed his eyes tightly and thumped his forehead with his fist. "Oh, no." He looked at his watch. "I haven't got time to stand here and argue. I have to shower and get to the airport."

"You have a shower?" It wasn't fair. The man had everything.

Casey raised his eyebrows. "Does that interest you?"

"Not in the least."

"Uh-huh." He slung his sleeping bag over his shoulder. "I'll leave you the pillow and the flashlight." He turned and walked toward his house, stopped short, muttered an expletive and returned to her. The expression on his face was an incongruous mixture of pain and laughter. He traced a line along her cheek with one finger and lowered his mouth to hers.

The kiss was gentle, a meeting of warm lips and fragile emotions. Alex felt little prickles of pleasure race through her stomach.

"I forgot to say good morning," Casey murmured against her slightly parted lips.

Alex swayed slightly. "Mmmmmm."

Casey grinned. "My cat sounds like that when I open a can of tuna fish." He tugged at a brown curl. "Listen, why don't you come up to the house with me and have a cup of coffee? I really do have to get to the airport. You could start the coffeepot going while I take a fast shower."

Coffee? That was playing hardball. She could find the strength to refuse a shower, but coffee . . . she'd kill for a cup of coffee. She could already smell the aroma, see the swirl of steam rising from the hot mug. Suddenly her very life seemed to depend on a cup of coffee. "Maybe a cup of coffee would be okay."

Casey took Alex's hand and pulled her toward his house. "After I leave, you can sit and have a nice quiet breakfast and take a hot shower."

Take her clothes off in Casey's house? Not a chance. She didn't care if he was in Timbuktu;

the thought of standing naked in Casey's shower gave her goose bumps. "I don't need a shower."

He looked at the snarled hair and dust-smudged face and grinned. She was stubborn and independent, she still didn't trust him and she wanted to get married. Damned if he knew why he liked her so much.

Three

Alex followed Casey through the birches and found herself standing knee-high in a broad lawn gone to seed. Last-of-the-season poppies struggled for sunlight amidst tall grass on a hill that sloped up toward a large log structure that seemed perfect for its environment. Built with massive yellow logs, it sat with its back to the hillside, its roof soaring toward the brilliant morning sky. Prowlike two-story windows faced the barely visible Alaska Range, and a redwood deck, cluttered with fishing gear and pots of flowers, encircled the building.

Alex stepped into the spacious house and looked around with a mixture of emotions, not the least of which was envy. The house had been built on one level with vaulted ceilings and exposed log walls that glowed mellow gold in the sunlight. The southern wall was entirely glass, giving a spectacular view of the valley and faraway mountains. An ornate silver and black potbellied woodstove sat on a red brick pad in the middle of the living-dining room area. It was flanked by built-in brick wood bins and backed by a floor-to-ceiling brick chimney. The floor was covered by plush wall-to-wall cocoa-colored carpet. The furniture was sparse—a large, comfortable-looking, plump couch, matching easy chair and a massive coffee table. It was clearly a man's furniture, but it was in excellent taste and suited the rugged sophistication of the room. The dining alcove held a round oak table and four intricately carved oak chairs, each different from the other. The small modern kitchen opened to the living-dining area, separated only by a butcher-block work island.

"It's nice," Alex told Casey.

"It's a little messy. I wasn't expecting company."

Alex swallowed at the understatement. Newspapers lay strewn across the living room floor. Empty beer cans adorned bookshelves, wood bins, window sills, and joined the loose change, used socks, and half-filled coffee cups on the coffee table. The kitchen counters were stacked with groceries that hadn't been put away. They sat side by side with unwashed dishes and bowls of bloated cereal in curdled milk. Alex peered into an encrusted pot and shivered involuntarily.

"Macaroni and cheese," he said. "I'm trying to decide whether to wash it or throw it away."

"How long have you been trying to decide? There's green furry stuff growing in here."

Casey shrugged and dismissed the issue with a glance at his watch. "I'm running late. Could you make some breakfast while I shower?"

Alex gingerly pushed the clutter away from the coffeepot. "I suppose that would be okay."

"Two eggs over easy, orange juice, coffee, English muffin."

Alex warily looked at the refrigerator and wondered what surprises it held. More green furry stuff? Rotting chickens? Potatoes au slime? She opened the door cautiously and was relieved to find unspoiled food. She took inventory of her surroundings as she broke the eggs into the one remaining clean frying pan and dropped a muffin into the toaster. Casey had good equipment. The appliances were all top of the line—pot-scrubber dishwasher, a refrigerator that flashed digital messages and talked, a garbage disposal, trash compactor, food processor, gas stove with barbeque, and microwave. The man was loaded all right. And a slob.

Six pots of dead African violets lined the windowsill. Alex felt the dirt. Dry as a bone. She watered the dead flowers and carefully flipped the eggs. She looked dismally at the sink half-filled with cold greasy water. A swollen bread crust floated amidst other culinary flotsam. Alex made a face and stuck her arm into the water to pull the plug. "Yuk."

She washed her hands, then slid the eggs and

muffin onto a plate just as Casey appeared in the kitchen doorway. He wore tailored black slacks that accentuated his slim hips and fell gracefully to a pair of expensive Italian leather loafers. Alex turned her attention to the tanned skin left exposed by his open shirt. A thatch of reddish-brown hair covered his chest and dipped in a slender line down to a flat muscular stomach. The hair darkened and swirled tantalizingly around his navel and slipped under the waistband of his slacks, leaving Alex to wonder about the ultimate destination of that enticing silken trail. She plunked the plate on the table with an appreciative sigh.

Casey buttoned the crisp white shirt and straddled a chair. "Aren't you eating?"

"Just coffee."

He buttered his muffin and looked at her thoughtfully. "Why did you buy that piece of land from old Harry?"

Alex slouched in her chair. "I don't know. One day I was Alexandra Scott, career woman, urban single, and then all of a sudden, I was on the road to Alaska." She sipped at her coffee. "Have you always lived in Alaska?"

Casey drained his glass of orange juice and nodded. "I went to school in California for a while, but I hated it."

"College?"

"Berkeley. I think I set a record. I went through seven different majors in four years."

"What did you finally graduate with?"

"Never graduated. In my senior year I decided I'd rather go fishing than take exams, so I left."

"I suppose rich people can do that sort of thing."

Casey chewed his muffin leisurely. "I wasn't rich. I was poor. After college I went to work on the pipeline until I'd saved enough money to buy a big old plane. I started doing produce runs from California to Fairbanks, and it all worked out pretty well." He reached for the coffeepot and filled their mugs. "I have a feeling you're avoiding my original question."

Alex sighed and rested her elbows on the table. "You want me to spill my guts, huh? It's very simple. It has to do with my biological clock. It's running out."

Casey looked at her solemnly. "Uh-huh."

"I'm going to be thirty years old in January. Thirty years old and I've never been married."

Casey's face flushed under his tan. "You don't mean you're a . . . you mean you've never . . ."

"That's not what I mean! I mean I've never been married. I've had a few boyfriends, but my career has kept me busy."

"So, you've been too busy to . . . ah—" Casey waved his half-eaten muffin "—have boyfriends."

Alex glared at him and tapped a teaspoon on the table. "The point is that I'm almost thirty, and I'm not married. My biological clock is ticking. Pretty soon it will be too late for me to get married and have kids."

"What's all this got to do with Alaska?"

"Women are grossly outnumbered here. It'll be

easier to find a husband." Alex leaned across the table in her enthusiasm. "And another thing. I want a healthy, caring man to father my children. I don't want some anxiety-ridden executive who's been sucking in pollution for the better part of his life."

Casey choked on his muffin. He put his napkin to his mouth and blurted, "How romantic. What do you do—take a sperm count and ask for a psychological profile before going out on a date?"

Alex settled back in her chair and watched him. He thought all this was pretty funny. He obviously didn't lie awake at night feeling lonely and wishing there was someone to talk to besides a dog. He didn't watch the babies in the supermarket and marvel at their little toes and chubby hands, and ache to kiss their downy soft hair and smooth cheeks. How dare he pass judgment on her needs. "Okay, so how does your spec sheet read for the future Mrs. Casey? How are you going about choosing a partner?"

Casey drained his cup and stood. "I don't have a spec sheet." He finished buttoning his shirt. "I'm not interested in finding a partner."

"Not at all?"

Casey pushed newspapers aside and uncovered a slim black attaché case from the coffee table. "Not at all."

"I suppose that's just as well because you're not my type, you know. You're all wrong."

"Lucky me. No offense, but I think you're a fruitcake." A delicious, desirable fruitcake, he silently added. He checked the contents of his brief-case, snapped it closed, threw his jacket over his arm and grabbed a set of keys from a small hook on the wall. "I'll be back late this evening."

He stood with his hand on the sliding glass door, staring down at the thick brown carpet while he fought with his emotions. "Oh, hell," he finally muttered, turning and reaching out for Alex. He pulled her toward him, crushing her breasts against his chest, forcing her thighs to slide eroti-cally between his legs. In an instant his mouth was on hers in an urgent, demanding kiss. His tongue teased hers, and he felt fire surge through him, burning with hungry desire.

He broke from the kiss, held Alex at arm's length and pressed his lips together in exasperation. "Promise me you won't get lost in the woods or eaten by a bear while I'm gone."

"Neither of those things was at the top of my list," she said. "I'm going to start working on my cabin."

He thought that sounded safe enough as long as she didn't use power tools or sharp objects. He retrieved his briefcase and jacket. "Help yourself to whatever you need here." He kissed her on the tip of her nose and left.

Alex watched him drive away. She licked her lips and took a deep breath. "Shoot. Must have been caffeine that made my heart race. Look at this, Bruno, my hands are shaking. See what too much coffee can do to you. Good thing you don't drink it."

She put the dishes in the dishwasher and followed the short hallway to Casey's bedroom. She found its decor to be similar to the rest of the house—early slob. One corner of the room was devoted to ski equipment. A bench and weights sat in the middle of the floor. An oak night table was littered with empty yogurt cups, dirty spoons, a crushed beer can, a red wool scarf, a copy of *Penthouse*, an enormous blue jogging shoe, and a newspaper section folded to the crossword puzzle. An oak chest sported the same sort of mess.

Alex smiled at the unmade double bed. Casey had obviously done a lot of thrashing about before deciding to join her in the tent. Either that or he hadn't made the bed in three weeks. A skylight had been installed in the ceiling above the bed, and it sent smoky shafts of sunlight streaming down on the rumpled comforter and jumble of sheets. An alcove had been added to the southern side of the room to house an impressive computer setup. Again, there were windows overlooking the Alaska Range. Casey could work at the computer and watch the sun travel across the sky. A CB radio system shared the alcove with the computer.

Bruno prowled after Alex. He inched his massive body under the bed and retrieved an empty container of chicken nuggets. He slid under one more time and presented Alex with an aromatic pizza box and a slinky black silk teddy.

Alex plucked the piece of lingerie from Bruno's mouth and held it at arm's length with one finger. "Look at this. I ask you, Bruno, what sort of woman would leave without her underwear. Yuk." Alex carefully placed the teddy in the pizza box, instinctively knowing that they belonged together.

Then she caught a glimpse of herself in the mirror over Casey's dresser and almost screamed out loud. She looked like a bag lady in a forty-five dollar sweatshirt. Her face was filthy, and her hair stood straight out. The electrocuted look, she grimly acknowledged. Casey was right—she needed a shower.

Half an hour later she marched into the kitchen feeling squeaky clean and ready for a day's work. "Breakfast is the most important meal of the day," she told Bruno. "Alexandra Scott, upwardly mobile career woman, could get away with a bagel and coffee at ten o'clock. Alexandra Scott, wilderness woman, needs a hearty breakfast at—" she looked at her watch and groaned "—seven-thirty."

She poured a bowl of granola and stared at it. "Nothing moving," she observed. She pushed the raisins around with her spoon and mashed the toasted oats into the sea of milk. She sniffed it suspiciously. It smelled okay, but it was hopeless. She couldn't eat it. Her stomach wasn't ready for Casey's granola. She pushed the bowl to one side, promising her body that she would treat it better tomorrow. Today she managed to pour the cereal and swill it around a bit, tomorrow she would try eating it. She looked at the desperate rottweiler sitting at tableside. "Do you like granola?" Of course he likes granola, she thought. He likes everything, anything. The dog would eat lint.

After Bruno had lapped up the last drop of milk, Alex went in search of tools. First priority would be to get the boards off the windows and let some air circulate through the little cabin. She selected a hammer and a small crowbar from the impressive array of equipment neatly hung on pegboards in Casey's garage. "What do you think, Bruno? Does this look like window-opening stuff?"

Three hours later she was sweating profusely, had broken three nails and ripped a hole in her designer jeans, but had all the windows open. Inside she assessed the thick wooden table occupying the middle of the floor and decided it was a hopeless eyesore. "Fred Flintstone furniture," she said, putting her weight behind it, pushing and pulling until it was outside, sitting next to the discarded shutters. She sagged against the table and swatted mosquitoes, her upper lip curling at the thought of her next task. She was going to have to get rid of the moldy mattress.

She cautiously approached the loft, kicking a path through the sawdust and cotton batting strewn on the floor. She held her breath, gritted her teeth, took a firm grip on the rotting material and pulled. In an instant the mattress was swarming with mice. Some jumped off the loft and fled, others ran helter-skelter across the mattress in panic. One bared its teeth and rose on its little haunches. Alex felt her eyes glaze over while she stood rooted to the spot in silent horror. One scurried across her sneakers, breaking the spell, sending her screaming out of the cabin. She didn't stop running until she was standing in the middle of Casey's kitchen. She took a cold beer from the refrigerator and sank into the nearest chair. "Holy cow."

"That's pretty strong language."

"Casey?"

He closed the patio door behind him and pitched his briefcase onto an overstuffed chair. "I pulled in just as you came barreling across the lawn. What the hell was after you? A bear?"

"Mice."

"Mice? Must have been a whole herd of them to get you to move like that."

"More like a cabinful." She took a swig of beer and rested the cold can against her flushed forehead. "They took me by surprise, but now it's war. I'll get the little devils."

Casey's eyes crinkled with laughter as he loosened his tie. "You're pretty brave for a broad from New Jersey."

"You think living in New Jersey is a piece of cake? You should see the rats in the New York subway system. You should try holding your own with an eighteen wheeler on the New Jersey Turnpike. Try getting a saleslady to wait on you in Bamberger's the week before Christmas."

"Boy, you really get steamed about New Jersey."

"I'm pumping myself up for the mice in my cabin. What are you doing home? I thought you weren't coming home until tonight?"

"The meeting was cancelled—by me. I couldn't stop worrying about you, so I came home."

"You didn't have to do that."

"I did. There's no one else on this mountain. If you broke your leg or sawed off a finger, you could yell all day and no one would hear you. You don't know anything about wilderness living or arctic survival. It's dangerous for you to be here alone."

"Oh, pooh."

Casey stared at her, dumbfounded. He didn't have an answer for "Oh, pooh." In fact, he didn't have an answer for anything anymore. His brain told him Alexandra Scott was a big girl, perfectly capable of taking care of herself, but his heart told him she needed to be protected. He was hopelessly infatuated with the woman, he was acting like a damn fool, and it seemed beyond his ability to change either.

"Did you really come home just because you were worried about me?"

"That was part of it. What really brought me home was the kiss."

Alex felt her stomach flip. "Well, you can stop thinking about it. There'll be no more kisses." She pushed herself away from the table and deposited the empty beer can in the trash masher.

"What do you mean, no more kisses? You don't just kiss a man like that and then say no more."

"You're all wrong, and you're going to mess everything up for me if we keep kissing like that."

"Why am I all wrong? I don't feel wrong. I feel just right."

"Do you want to get married?"

"No."

"Then you're all wrong," Alex said.

"Why can't we fool around a little?"

"I don't fool around."

Casey opened the top button of his shirt. "How did I know that?"

Alex smiled at his tone of grudging admiration. It would be easy to fall in love with Michael Casey, but she wasn't going to allow herself that pleasure if he wasn't interested in marriage. She'd come to Alaska with a definite purpose, and she wouldn't be dissuaded from it. She grabbed a can of Raid and tucked a broom under her arm. "Death to bugs and mice."

Casey grimaced. "Give me a minute to change my clothes, and I'll be down to help you."

At seven P.M. Alex leaned against Casey's, 4x4 Ford pickup and wondered if her back would ever be the same. The vertebrae no longer fit together. Tennis and aerobic dancing obviously used a different set of muscles than cabin cleaning.

Casey tossed one last board into the back of the truck and joined Alex. "You look beat."

"Just pacing myself."

He watched her thoughtfully. "Why are you really doing this? It's hard to believe you couldn't find a husband in New Jersey. And why this cabin?" he said, gesturing to the little hut. "This is going to be so tough on you. Why don't you get something more civilized?"

Alex closed her eyes and pushed her hair away from her face. "The truth is, I couldn't get a man in New Jersey. I had no time. I had an eighty thousand dollar a year dream job working for a brokerage firm in Manhattan. I got up every morning at four-thirty so I could take a shower, put on makeup, and rush to catch the train from Princeton to New York. I got back to Princeton at seven o'clock at night, ate a box of Oreos and drank a glass of one-percent milk, fed Bruno and went to bed. On weekends I did my laundry, cleaned my house, shopped for next week's Oreos, and wondered how much longer I could keep going. I owned a hundred and fifty-five thousand dollar condo, filled with beautiful furniture and Waterford crystal . . . and I traded it for this!" She tipped her head back and laughed. "I know it sounds crazy, but I absolutely don't give a fig about all that crystal."

"You traded it? Are you serious?"

"Yup. Old Harry is probably burning cigar holes in my Drexel dining room table right now."

"Did you do this legally? With lawyers and papers and stuff?"

"It's not as bad as it seems. I got his business too. He got my house and the remainder of my mortgage payments, and I got this land and his hardware store. I know it's just a small store, but I had almost no equity in the house. Even my lawyer finally had to admit that it might not be such a bad trade."

"Have you seen the store yet?"

"No. Oh, don't tell me!" Alex sprang from the truck. "Don't tell me the store is a bust too."

"Not at all. But it's not exactly a hardware store.

It's more of a hunting and fishing store with a few nuts and bolts lying around. You like to fish?"

Alex gave him a blank look.

"Let me guess. You've never been fishing."

"How difficult can it be? You just sell hooks and things. And it'll be a great way to meet . . . people."

"Oh, yeah, the boring brown-haired guy who wants to get married." Casey shook his head. "Boring guys are smarter than you think. No boring guy in his right mind would marry a woman with hair like this." He playfully tugged at a dusty, renegade curl. "Only a man with a strong sense of adventure would even consider marrying you. And a sense of humor wouldn't hurt either."

"My hair doesn't usually look like this. Usually it's very nice."

Casey remembered her standing on the ramp in Juneau when her hair had been burnished by the morning sun and thought nice wasn't even close. Her hair was glorious, luxuriant, extravagant, sexy. Definitely sexy, even in its present condition of disarray. And rumpled, he thought, like it would be after a night of loving. An image of the lush auburn hair spread across his pillow caused a rush of desire to knot his stomach. He firmly pushed the fantasy from his mind and took the truck keys from his pocket. "We've done about all we can with the cabin. Tomorrow I'll work on your driveway with the chain saw. I can clear it out, but you'll never be able to drive that little red car on it. You're going to have to either put in a load of stone or else get a four-wheel drive."

"That sounds expensive."

Casey looked sideways at her. "Don't tell me you haven't any money."

"I'm sort of on a budget. I have money set aside for the store, and I have a little money for cabin necessities, like an outhouse. This hasn't turned out exactly as I'd planned."

"You don't seem too upset about it."

"I know. Isn't that amazing?"

Casey nodded. "Amazing. Get in the truck."

"Where are we going?"

"Home." .

"This is *my* home."

"This is not *anybody's* home. This is a cabin that reeks of insecticide and mold killer. This is a tent that has been pitched downhill on a rock slide." He pointed to his house with his finger. "That is home. That is a comfortable house with running water and furniture and food. Maybe by the end of the week this cabin will be habitable. In the meantime, you can stay with me."

Stay with Casey? He had a toaster, and a dustbuster, and an automatic icemaker. Very tempting. He also had a smile that made her crazy. She could eventually tear herself away from the appliances, but that smile could be addicting. She stiffened her spine. "I think I'll just rough it out here," she said, trying to sound enthusiastic.

"You're looney tunes."

"Independent," she said, raising her chin a fraction of an inch.

Casey looked at the sky. "This isn't a good time to be independent. It's going to rain."

"I like rain. Go away."

Casey's mouth tightened at her determination. She was impossible. She made him nuts. It would serve her right if she got eaten by a bear. He'd give her until nine o'clock, and then. . . . And then he didn't know what he'd do! He got into his truck and drove off, crushing the highbush cranberries and pine saplings under his oversized wheels.

A drop of rain fell on Alex's nose. Great. She didn't need rain. What she *did* need was to soak in a hot tub. She needed to slip a Fred Astaire movie into the VCR and relax on a comfy couch. She needed to strangle Harry. She thought of *The Wizard of Oz* and how water had melted the Wicked Witch of the West. That's how she felt, like the Wicked Witch of the West, and the rain was making her cranky and melting all her good intentions.

"Damn! Ugh!" She viciously kicked at the tent, knocking loose a stake and bending one of the supporting struts. She glared at the dented dome and attempted to straighten it, only to have the whole tent collapse. Oh, boy, she thought, now she'd really done it. She didn't have a clue how to get the tent back together. But that was fine, she wasn't crazy about it anyway.

"Good thing we have a cabin," she told Bruno. She fished inside the tent until she found her sleeping bag. "This will be great. Our first night in our new home." Bruno stopped at the threshold and refused to go in. Alex stood in the middle of the little house and gasped. Casey was right— the cabin reeked of insecticide. "Okay," she fumed, stomping outside, "we'll sleep under the stars." More rain plopped on her forehead and softly pattered on the tin roof. Bruno wrinkled his nose in disgust, turned his back on his mistress and trotted along the path leading to Casey's house.

"Traitor. Dumb, stupid, fat dog," Alex shouted after him. She looked at the soggy tent. Rain dripped off the tip of her nose. Who was she kidding? She moaned. The dog was smarter than she.

Minutes later, Alex stood on Casey's deck in silent resignation. Not only was she forced to humiliate herself by begging for his help after she had refused his hospitality, but she was disgusting. Her sneakers squished when she walked. She had fallen twice on the slippery, muddy path and skinned her knee. Her hair was plastered against her face and neck in dark ringlets, and her drenched green silk shirt clung to her like a second skin. Alex gazed through the patio door at Casey and Bruno watching TV in front of a cozy fire. She rolled her eyes in exasperation and rapped on the glass.

"Well, if it isn't Alexandra Scott," Casey exclaimed in mock surprise. His eyes dropped to the bloody knee, and the color drained from his face. "Ye gods, woman, what happened to you?"

"I accidentally collapsed my dumb tent, and then I fell on your dumb trail."

"I never should have left you down there alone." He pulled her into the house and closed the door. "How bad is your knee?"

Alex narrowed her eyes at the scolding tone of his voice. "I would have been fine if it hadn't been for a bizarre series of minor catastrophes."

Casey scooped her into his arms and held her tight against his chest as he carried her into the bathroom. "I don't know what your life was like in New Jersey, but it seems to me ever since you set foot on Alaskan soil you've been a walking disaster. And now look what you've done to your knee. With my luck it's probably broken, and I'll have you thumping around my house in a cast for nine months."

"It's not broken. It's only a scratch, and even if it was broken, I wouldn't thump around in your house. I didn't come all these miles to waste my time living with a man who doesn't want to marry me." She tried to push away from him. "Put me down!"

He tightened his grip on her. "Stop squirming."

"It's not necessary for you to carry me. I'm fine."

Casey stopped in midstride and looked at her. "You really don't want to be carried?"

"Yes. No." Now that she thought about it, it was pretty nice being carried. He was strong and muscular, and his warmth passed through her thin shirt and traveled straight to the pit of her stomach. She put her hand to his shirt. "I can feel your heart beating."

"My heart is not beating. My heart is racing. You make me crazy." He set her on the bathroom vanity top and examined her knee through the gaping hole in her jeans. "I feel like an idiot. Twenty-four hours ago I was a perfectly contented bachelor, and now . . ." He reached behind him and turned on the shower. "Now I don't know what I am!"

"It's probably just a testosterone attack."

"Lady, I've had testosterone attacks before. This is testosterone war."

Alex shivered and clenched her teeth to keep from chattering. "Ccccold."

Casey removed her sneakers and pitched them into the corner of the bathroom. "Go stand in the shower until you're warm and wrinkled. I'll make some coffee." His eyes softened as he looked down at her. "Don't suppose you'd want me to scrub your back?"

"I can scrub my own back, thank you. I told you before, you're all wrong."

He kissed her softly on the lips. "Maybe."

Alex watched him leave and locked the door behind him. Maybe? What was that supposed to mean? She didn't like the sound of his maybe, she thought. It sounded too much like maybe not, which was practically the same as not being wrong at all. She threw her wet clothes in the corner with her sneakers and climbed into the steamy shower. Her life was going down the drain like this water, she decided. Nothing was going right. It kept getting worse and worse. Even her dog had abandoned her.

Alex let the hot water splash against her neck. She lathered the mud away and washed her hair and stood in the shower until she was as red as a lobster. When she was totally relaxed and thoroughly toasty she wrapped herself in a huge fluffy white towel and pondered her predicament. She had no clothes. Casey was in the kitchen, brewing coffee and warming his libido, and she was trapped in the bathroom—naked.

Four

Alex clutched the towel to her chest and peeked around the bathroom door. "Casey?" No answer. She made sure the towel was wrapped as securely as possible, and cautiously made her way to the kitchen.

Casey grinned when he saw her. He put the lid on the drip coffeepot and inspected her from the tip of her toes to the top of her head. She reminded him of pink-frosted birthday cake—sweet, tempting, and totally edible. "You look delicious," he said. "I'm glad you're not hiding all that rosy skin under clothes."

"I seem to be in an embarrassing situation here. My clothes are all wet."

Casey set a bag of cookies and two mugs of coffee on the coffee table. He took a soft blue blanket from the couch and wrapped it around

Alex. "Now you can drop your towel, and you'll be modestly and warmly clad in this nifty blanket. As soon as we're done with our cookies and coffee, I'll slog my way down to your tent for some clothes. Deal?"

"Deal." She dropped the towel and immediately knew she had made a mistake. The lightly abrasive blanket fell in caressing folds on skin sensitized by the hot shower. She felt the tips of her breasts peak under the slight friction, and almost groaned out loud as it rubbed against her belly and slid between her thighs when she sat on the couch.

Casey grinned at her. "Feel better?"

She was going to get him for this, she decided. He knew *exactly* how she felt. This was probably how he tricked that poor girl out of her black silk teddy. She tentatively perched on the edge of the couch and nibbled at a cookie. "It's not going to work."

"It's not?"

"Nope. My mind is made up about what I want, and I'm not going to compromise." She sipped her coffee and took another cookie.

Casey slouched into a corner of the couch and looked at her over the rim of his coffee mug. "I have to be honest—I'm very attracted to you. Half of me wants to seduce that blanket off you, and the other half is making me feel guilty as hell because I have no intention of marrying you."

"Listen to the half that feels guilty. The other half wouldn't have any luck anyway. I told you before, you're not what I'm looking for. I want someone extremely stable, someone who loves children, someone with small appetites and some common sense in his genes."

"That sure as hell leaves me out. I've been having problems with my jeans ever since I met you, and damned if I can find any sense in it." He swallowed the last of his coffee and stood up, feeling impatient and irritable. Someone with small appetites, he thought disgustedly. Didn't she know anything at all about herself? Anyone with half a brain could see she was not a woman with small appetites. What did she think she was going to do with an indifferent man? She'd go nuts. And she'd probably turn him into a raving lunatic.

"Are we talking about the same kind of genes?"

"I don't know. I could think a lot more clearly if you weren't wearing that blanket."

"This blanket was your idea."

"Yeah, and it was a stupid one." He crossed the room and grabbed a yellow slicker from a hook on the wall. "I'm going to get your clothes."

Alex curled her feet under her and stared into the crackling fire. Casey was very tempting. He was movie-star handsome, and he oozed sexuality. The thought of going to bed with him almost took her breath away. But she didn't travel five thousand miles for a roll in the hay, she reminded herself. She was a woman who set high goals and worked hard to attain them. She'd gotten her vice presidency because she'd aggressively pursued it, and she'd get the husband she wanted the same way.

The fire hissed hypnotically in the quiet house, and rain drummed on the roof. Alex stretched out on the couch and closed her eyes, allowing herself a few minutes of rest before Casey returned.

Alex opened her eyes to the morning aroma of bacon frying and coffee brewing. She was still on the couch, and she was still wrapped in the blue blanket, but a down comforter had been tucked in around her, and a pillow had been put under her head. She propped herself up on one elbow to get a better view of Casey working in the kitchen.

He moved quietly in stockinged feet and whispered to Bruno as he worked. "Just one piece of bacon for you, Bruno, and don't tell your mistress. You should be on a diet."

Alex clutched the blanket to her and walked toward the kitchen. "I heard that. You're sweet, but devious." She unsuccessfully tried to suppress a smile when she saw Casey wearing an apron.

He raised an eyebrow at the smile. "Are you laughing at my apron?"

Alex bit her lip.

"Go ahead and laugh. You look like you're ready to rupture something."

"It just caught me by surprise," Alex said, grinning broadly.

Casey poked at the bacon with a long fork. "I'm a real threat in the kitchen. Last time I cooked bacon, I set my pants on fire. I figured an apron was easier to get off just in case I went up in flames again."

"Goodness. Hope you didn't damage anything important."

Casey laughed softly. "No, I didn't damage anything important. And it's nice to know you're concerned."

Alex took a piece of bacon from the paper towel on the counter. "Just making conversation."

"Uh-huh."

She'd been caught flirting with him. Drat. She tightened the blanket and munched on her bacon slice. "The coffee smells terrific."

Casey put the frying pan on a back burner and removed his apron. "You can have some as soon as you get dressed. I don't think I can manage being a gentleman too much longer, knowing you're naked under that."

"I guess I fell asleep before you got back last night."

"Yeah. It's becoming painfully obvious why you've had such limited experience with boyfriends."

"Have I just been insulted?"

"Not only do you instill feelings that discourage casual seduction, but you fall asleep at the drop of a hat." He gestured with the long fork. "Your backpack is in my bedroom."

Alex narrowed her eyes. The nerve of the man insinuating that she wasn't stimulating company! "It was a long day, and I'm not used to being attacked by rabid mice, and I practically broke my knee—"

"Scott?"

"Yeah?"

"Go get dressed."

With an imperial toss of her head, she turned around and headed for the bedroom. She quickly donned a pair of pale gray, lightweight wool slacks and a matching cashmere sweater. She accented the outfit with an orange, black, and gray scarf and slid her feet into a pair of delicate black, lizard skin penny loafers. She was trying to tame her hair when Casey walked in.

He stood just behind her and stared at her reflection in the mirror. She looked beautiful, like someone out of a New York fashion magazine—about as un-Alaskan as a person could get. He reached out to touch a chestnut curl and stopped himself. Off limits, he thought. This woman was heartbreak city. He was falling in love with her, and she was going to leave. No one who wore shoes like that stayed in Alaska for very long. So what was the problem, he asked himself. Wasn't that what he wanted? A little romance without the long-term commitment of marriage and family? "You look very pretty," he finally said. "What were you planning on doing today?"

"Shopping. I need some household things, and I'm anxious to see my store."

Casey looked at her little black shoes and shook his head. "I've never known anyone who carried fancy clothes like this in a backpack."

"Wool and silk are wonderful for traveling if you roll them properly." She put her hair back in a big gold clip. "And I got these shoes for half price in Bloomingale's. I thought they'd be good for Alaska because they have low heels."

Casey looked at her nonplussed. She was serious. "Alex," he said gently, "you live on a mountain in the boonies. Your car is three miles away through the woods."

Alex considered the shoes. She had more rugged clothes, but they were coming by mail. She'd only been able to fit a few bare essentials in her small car. "You think I need something more sturdy?"

"Just a tad." He slung his arm around her shoulder and propelled her toward the kitchen. "Let's have breakfast, and then I think we'll go shopping together. Uncle Casey is going to get you properly outfitted."

Terrific, Alex thought. His idea of properly outfitted was probably pasties and a garter belt.

"Stop grinning like that," Alex said, poking Casey in the ribs.

"I can't help it. I've never seen a toilet seat done in fake leopard skin before. Feel this thing. It's furry. This is just what you need for those cold winter nights when you have to make a trip to the outhouse."

"Don't remind me. If I'd known about the outhouse part, I probably would have stayed in New Jersey."

Casey took a boxed toilet seat from the display. "Look, it's a bargain. Only $37.50, reduced from $45."

"I don't have $37.50 to lavish on an endangered species toilet seat. I can get a nice plastic one for $12."

"You know what it's like to sit on a plastic toilet seat at thirty degrees below zero?"

Alex reached for her wallet. This was getting expensive. Casey was staggering under a burden of bags, most of which were filled with items she hadn't intended to buy. Long underwear, thick woolen socks, hiking boots that looked as if they were made for Herman Munster, an air horn to scare off bears since she'd refused to buy a gun, and a heavy-duty red and black plaid wool shirt.

"Tell you what," Casey said, "I'll give you this toilet seat as a present. I have to give you something to welcome you to my mountain. It's an old Alaskan custom."

"Oh, ha!"

"You're cute when you say that. Do you think anyone would notice if I kissed you?"

Alex jumped back. "Don't you come near me."

Casey grinned. He liked it when he could rattle her a little and her eyes widened in startled uncertainty. He was beginning to know some of her behavior patterns. The startled uncertainty wouldn't last long. It would be immediately followed by compressed lips and narrowed eyes in a brief flash of anger as she regained her composure. Alexandra Scott liked being in control. "Why don't you go look at curtains," Casey said. "I'll join you as soon as I pay for this."

Ten minutes later Casey found Alex in front of a display of white ruffled Martha Washington style curtains.

"Cabins are supposed to have curtains like this," Alex told him. "I know because I read *Little House on the Prairie* three times. And I watch television. I think they had curtains like this on *Bonanza*. And besides, these curtains are cheap."

"Those curtains will look great with your new comforter."

Alex looked at him warily. "I don't have a new comforter."

"Yes, you do." He pushed a huge bag in her direction. "It's red. It's an old Alaskan custom that if you give someone a gift they hate, you also have to give them something nice."

"I don't hate the toilet seat. I think it will be sort of . . . invigorating."

Casey grinned. "The quilt will be even more invigorating."

Alex had an involuntary mental picture of Casey cuddling next to her under the red quilt. She felt her face flush hot and smiled guiltily.

Casey watched the pulse jump in her neck. He lay his hand against her blushing cheek, and lightly brushed his thumb across her full lower lip. He was being a real crumb, and he was going to get even crummier, he thought ruefully. He wanted Alex, and he was about to begin a campaign to get what he wanted. His good intentions and virtuous morals paled in comparison to his desire for her.

Two hours later, Alex grimly smiled at the small cache of furniture and household goods piled into the back of Casey's pickup. A chest of drawers, a card table, two chairs. "A little modest by Princeton standards," she said, nervously smoothing an imaginary wrinkle from her slacks.

Casey stopped for a light on the two-lane highway connecting Fairbanks and College. "Having regrets?"

"No. This is scary, but it's fun. I can't wait to see my store."

"It's just ahead on the right-hand side."

Alex looked, but there were no shopping centers in sight. Scrubby fields bordered either side of the road, the ground being too thin to support the lush vegetation found in the southern part of the state. A clapboard bungalow shored up with scrap metal from jerry cans and pieces of plastic hunkered off the shoulder. Two antique gas pumps stood sentinel on the cracked cement pad in front of the building. A weathered wooden sign advertising live bait had been propped against one of the pumps. Alex drew her dark brows together in confusion. "I don't see anything that looks like a store."

"That's because you're looking for a New Jersey-type store." Casey pulled into a section of field that had been worn down to rutted dirt and parked beside the clapboard building. "This is an Alaskan-type store."

Alex looked at the building and felt the blood drain from her face. "This is a joke, isn't it?"

"Welcome to Harry's store."

"I think I'm going to be sick."

"It's not so bad. This is an excellent location. This road is well traveled, the university is just around the bend and the train tracks are on the other side of that stand of birches. The store has electricity and running water. It looks a little rough around the edges, but I think it could be very profitable if handled properly. Harry was content to just get by. If you put your mind to it, you could make money here. Of course, it would help if you knew something about what you were selling."

Alex sighed and heaved herself from the truck. "Okay, let's take a look inside."

Casey stopped her before they went in. "Did Harry tell you about Andy?"

"Andy Crump, Harry's clerk? Harry said Andy was keeping the store going for him. That's all he said."

"Kids call him Crump the Grump. He's been clerking this store for twenty years. Lives in a little room off the back."

Harry hadn't shared that information with Alex. "Does he pay rent?"

"No, and I wouldn't suggest that he begin. In fact, I'd go very slow with any kind of suggestions."

"You're trying to tell me something."

Casey draped his arm around her shoulders. "When we walk through this door, I want you to stay very calm. And it would be good if you found something nice to say about the store. You could comment on the knives in the display case by the register. You could tell Andy you thought they were arranged nicely."

"I don't like the sound of this."

Casey tugged at the door and stepped side for Alex to pass. "Just keep an open mind."

"An open mind," she repeated as she inspected her property, which consisted of a large rectangular room heated by an ornate potbellied stove around which stood a scarred redwood picnic table and several chairs.

"For the boys," Casey explained.

A huge dusty moosehead hung on a wall over an ancient cash register. A filthy glass display case housed a motley assortment of hunting and fishing knives and fishing reels. Small wooden boxes partially filled with rusting nuts and bolts and nails lined the long wall and cluttered the middle of the room. A bare bulb hung from an overhead fixture, but since the electricity had been turned off, the only illumination came from the light stealing through the grimy windows and open front door.

The disappointment was almost crushing. Harry had swindled her. The lawyer had been right. Intelligent people didn't go around buying property sight unseen. She could forgive the cabin, at least it had a view, but the store was unforgivable. "Do they sell guns here?" she asked Casey. "Suicide is beginning to have some appeal. Maybe I would slit my throat with one of those knives."

Casey's eyes crinkled with amusement. "You think you're depressed now? Wait until you meet Andy. This is nothing compared to him."

Alex turned from Casey to gather her wits together, feeling like a total fool. Tears were swarming in her eyes and she angrily blinked them away. The last thing she wanted to do was burst into tears like some weak, nitwit female. She crossed her arms over her chest and kicked at a keg of nails, then began prowling the room like a wounded lioness.

Casey saw the brightness in her eyes and swore softly. Damn that Harry. What the hell was he thinking, sending some New York fashion plate up here, leading her to think she was getting a fancy hardware store? He ran his hand through his hair. It wasn't Harry's fault. Harry loved his cabin and his store. He undoubtedly thought Alex was getting the better deal. In fact, maybe she was. The store actually was in a decent location, and it sat free and clear on a large piece of land that was going to become prime real estate someday.

Casey walked over to her and again slung his arm around her shoulders. "Alex, it's not as bad as you think. The ground this store sits on is going to be worth money."

"Is it worth money now?"

Casey made an exasperated sound. "I don't know. A little."

She closed her eyes and leaned against him. "Lord, I've made a mess of things."

He pressed his cheek against her silky hair, hating the store for not being what she'd expected, hating himself for falling in love with a gullible woman who would take off for warmer climes the minute the snow got to the tops of her shoes.

Alex pushed away from him and looked around the room. Now that the initial shock was wearing off, she began a more professional assessment of her situation. "Do you really think this is a good location?"

Casey was slow in answering. "Yes."

"Do you really think I could make money here?"

"I think *someone* could make money here. I'm not sure that someone is you." He leaned against the display case and crossed his arms over his chest while a small war was waged in his mind. She was in a hopeless situation, part of him said. Leave her alone, and she would be forced to pack her bags and go home to New Jersey. Better to get rid of her before he got too involved. The other part of him wanted her to stay. More than that, the other part of him wanted her to succeed. It took a lot of guts to uproot yourself and search for a better life. He respected her for that. And she'd worked side by side with him on the cabin yesterday and never complained, and then had the pluck to want to sleep in her tent. He respected her for that too. The war ended.

"I think there's a lot of potential here if you forget about the hardware and turn this place into an all-around sporting goods store. Hunting, fishing, backpacking, camping, cross-country skiing. But you're going to have to do it slowly. This place is sort of a watering hole for seniors and die-hard sourdoughs. If you make too many changes too fast you'll loose a bunch of steady customers. I know this place looks really bad to you, but if you're frugal, it'll probably support you through the winter. In the spring you can start beefing up your line of fishing gear."

Alex felt a smile creeping across her mouth. It wasn't much of a store, but it was hers. She'd do what Casey suggested, and next spring she'd begin to make improvements. "This is going to be great," she said to Casey. "I can do some cleaning, can't I?"

Casey shook his head. "The eternal optimist." He swiped a finger across the glass case of knives and looked disgustedly at the filth. "Yeah, you can. Andy's not going to like it, but what the hell."

Alex looked around. "Where is this Andy person?"

"Andy!" Casey shouted.

Alex could hear him mumbling before she saw him. "No need to yell," he said from the back room. "A body can't do nothin' around here without being disturbed." He was small and wiry with a gray stubbly beard and tufts of coarse gray hair sprouting from his ears and nose. His eyes were faded behind round spectacles, but they narrowed speculatively when they focused on Alex, and she had the impression that they didn't miss much.

His plaid flannel shirt was frayed at the collar but clean. Thermal underwear peeked from the open neck and showed through a small hole in the knee of his gray work pants. "Well?" he said to Casey. "What do you want?"

Casey made an attempt to look serious, but laughter was bubbling deep inside. This was going to be some combination. He didn't know if he felt more sorry for Alex or for Andy. "Andy, this is Alexandra Scott. I assume Harry's been in touch with you about selling the store?"

"Harry's a horse's rump."

Casey grinned broadly. "The ball's in your court," he whispered to Alex.

Alex extended her hand. "It's very nice to meet you, Andy. I'm sure you'll be a great help to me this winter while I'm learning about the, um, bait and tackle business."

"You aren't gonna be hanging around here, getting in my way, are you?"

Alex drew her shoulders back slightly. "Yes, as a matter of fact, I am," she said with cheerful authority. Casey raised his eyebrows in admiration, and Andy glared at her.

"Well, I ain't gonna be pushed around by some female who don't know squat," Andy said.

"Then I'll make an effort to learn squat as soon as possible." Alex moved to the case by the register. "This is a very nice display," she said, smiling at Andy. "Did you do this?"

Andy wasn't about to be bought off by a compliment. "Hmph," he said, standing his ground.

Alex looked at the unlit bulb hanging over her head. "It's dark in here. Why don't you turn the light on?"

"Ain't nobody in the store now. No reason to burn electricity."

"You turn the light on when customers come in?"

"If I think they're worth it."

Alex turned to Casey. "Makes perfect sense to me."

Casey stuffed his hands in his jeans pockets. "Me, too."

"Well, keep up the good work," Alex said to Andy. "I'll be in tomorrow to do some cleaning. Maybe we should close the store for the day."

"Don't need to do that. Won't be nobody in the store tomorrow anyway."

Alex let herself out and closed the door behind her. "Are you sure this is going to support me?" she asked Casey.

"Trust me."

"I'm getting rid of Andy."

"I wouldn't do that if I were you. Andy's what keeps this store in the black. He knows every-thing about hunting and fishing. People don't come here to buy. They come here to talk to Andy, and while they're here he gets them to buy stuff."

"Swell." It was only one word, but it combined the multitude of emotions she felt. Amusement, disgust, anger, determination.

Most people were intimidated by Andy, Casey thought, but Alex hadn't blinked an eye. He liked that. She was no pushover. Wall Street probably breathed a sigh of relief when she left. He found her easy assumption of authority to be oddly stimulating, and the challenge of holding his own with her sent a ripple of pleasure straight to his groin. His mouth twitched into a satisfied smile, and he pulled her to him for a long, hard kiss. It wasn't a sensuous, passionate kiss. It was impudent and possessive and very thorough. His voice was pleasantly raspy when he ended the kiss. "Nice."

Alex swayed toward him slightly. There was a sharp intake of breath when she realized he'd stopped kissing her, and she narrowed her eyes, just as he knew she would.

Casey had kissed her as if she were his private property. Not an attitude she appreciated since he'd made it clear he wasn't about to assume mortgage payments. She placed her fists onto her hips and glowered at him. "I'm glad you enjoyed it. It's going to be the last kiss you get from me."

"We'll see."

"What do you mean, we'll see?"

Casey grinned and tugged at a chestnut curl. "I like to kiss you. C'mon, let's attack that cabin of yours."

Alex was certain her back was broken. She had pain in muscles she never knew existed. And her nails were grotesque, she thought grimly. They were cracked and chipped, and the polish was peeling off. It was a good thing she was too tired to care, she decided.

But as she stood on the threshold of her cabin and surveyed her handiwork, she felt a burst of pride. Six hours of sanding and varnishing had produced a floor that was glistening clean and slick. The woodwork around the windows and the walls had received similar treatment. She hoped tomorrow everything would be dry so she could move her furniture in and hang curtains. Her life was now divided into two distinct segments—before sanding and after sanding.

Alex turned toward the sound of the chain saw whining deep in her driveway. Casey had been right—she wouldn't be able to drive her little car through until the gravel was laid, but at least the path looked more civilized now that Casey had leveled the vegetation. The saw sputtered to a stop, and Alex thought the sudden silence was filled with suspense, as if the mountain might be holding its breath. After a moment the world whooshed a sigh of relief. Air swished through the trees, and birds began chirruping songs in anticipation of night. Alex was suffused with pleasure at the sight of Casey and Bruno heading for her in the truck. They're coming to get me, she consoled herself. They're going to put the lid on my can of paint, and then they're going to take me up the hill to die in peace.

They stopped and got out. Casey walked over to her and pried the can of varnish from her sticky fingers. "You okay? You look kind of dopey." He hammered the lid down. "Looks to me like you passed tired about two hours ago."

"Not me. Us broads from New Jersey never get tired."

Casey shook his head and laughed softly. She was a sight, and she was out on her feet. "Do you think you can make it to the truck?"

"No sweat."

"I'd carry you, but you're covered head to foot with varnish. What did you do, roll in it?"

Alex looked at her spattered jeans. "It just sort of sprang from the brush onto me."

"I don't know whether I should put you in the front with Bruno and me, or just lay you out in the back."

Alex's shoulders sagged. "For all I care, you could drag me behind."

Casey tenderly kissed her on top of her head. "Poor Alex." He lifted her into the cab, wedging her between Bruno and the door to keep her propped up while he bumped along the rough, freshly cut "driveway."

When he pulled up in front of his house, she had a glazed expression on her face. Her eyes were open, but Casey wasn't sure she was awake. He gently eased her from the truck. "Here we go," he said. "You can do it. Just put one foot in front of the other." He opened the patio door and put his hand to the small of her back. "Not far now. Pretty soon you'll be standing in a nice warm shower."

"Mmmmm. Shower."

Casey led her down the hall and adjusted the water. "Are you going to be all right? Do you need help?"

"Don't need help."

"I'll make some soup."

"Soup," Alex parroted. She locked the door, dragged herself out of her clothes, climbed into the steaming shower and wondered where she would find the strength to wash her hair. She was still wondering when she heard Casey pounding on the bathroom door.

"You okay?" he called.

"Okay."

"You've been in there for twenty minutes."

Alex leaned her head against the tile wall. "I think I fell asleep."

"Maybe you should come out now."

Alex stepped out of the shower and wrapped herself in a towel. She opened the door. "I don't have any clothes."

"They're in the backpack in my bedroom."

"Oh, yeah."

Casey grinned down at her. "Good thing you're a tough tootsie from New Jersey. Imagine if you were some wimpy female from Virginia or Rhode Island."

"Good thing."

Casey pushed her into the bedroom. "Why don't you get into your Dr. Denton's and climb into bed, and I'll bring you some soup."

Alex rummaged through her clothes and put on purple cotton panties and an oversized Princeton

University T-shirt. She towel dried her hair and slid into bed, too tired to care about propriety, independence or modesty. It was Casey's bed, so what. Let him sleep on the couch. She closed her eyes and gave a satisfied groan as her bones relaxed into the mattress.

Casey returned, placed a bed tray on her lap and tucked a napkin into the neck of her T-shirt. "I made tomato soup and grilled cheese sandwiches."

"Looks great." Alex took a bite of sandwich. "I didn't realize how hungry I was."

"I should never have let you work that long."

"It wasn't your fault. I was the one who didn't want supper, and I was the one who wanted to finish the varnishing." Alex tasted the soup and sighed happily. "Yum."

"It's my specialty. I'm really good at opening cans." He nibbled a corner off her grilled cheese. "I don't suppose you're going to let me sleep with you tonight."

Alex gave him a light tap on the forehead with her soupspoon. "Get real."

"Thought there wasn't any harm in asking."

"Mmm, well, the answer is no."

Casey took a sip of the soup and chomped off a large bite of sandwich. "This is damn frustrating."

"You'll have to excuse me if I don't sound too sympathetic. My libido is definitely second in line to my stomach." She quickly gobbled the remainder of her sandwich and took possession of the soupspoon just as Casey was reaching for it. "Touch that soupspoon and you're a dead man."

Casey raised his eyebrows slightly and talked from the side of his mouth. "Better watch it, Buttercup, I'm the guy who's gonna plow your driveway this winter. And I'm the guy with the hot shower, the seven-cycle washer, and the power saw. Better be nice to me."

"What nerve. Instead of being embarrassed because you were snitching my supper, you threaten me with your middle-class appliances. And if that isn't bad enough, you do it with the worst impression of Bogart I've ever heard."

"Boy, that really hurt. And I was going to get you some ice cream too."

"Ice cream? Oh Casey, I'd *love* some ice cream. Is it chocolate?"

A slow, mocking smile stole across Casey's face. "I bet you'd do anything for chocolate ice cream."

Alex instinctively drew the covers up to her neck. "What did you have in mind?"

"Heh, heh, heh."

"Shame on you. That's horrible. That's the dirtiest laugh I've ever heard. You know how bad I want that ice cream!"

"Damn right!"

He was the most outrageous, endearing, disarming man she'd ever met. She tried to simulate a scowl. "Where are your scruples?"

"I think I left them in the kitchen."

"Well, you can retrieve them when you go out there to get me my ice cream."

Casey removed the bed tray and set it on the

floor. "I'll get you some ice cream if you'll give me a kiss."

"What kind of kiss? Are you talking about a big kiss or a little kiss?"

"A medium kind of kiss."

"Will there be other body parts involved in this kiss?" Alex asked, struggling to keep her voice stern. "Or is this just a lips' kiss?"

Casey's mouth curved in a devilish smile. "Feeling spunky, huh? Better not tease me too much, that ice cream is looking doubtful."

"This is an important decision. I need more information."

Casey sighed. "I suppose I'm going to have to take matters into my own hands." He watched her for a moment before leaning forward and claiming her mouth. His lips brushed across hers softly, testing the texture, enjoying her breathless expectation. Despite what she'd said back at the store, she'd wanted to be kissed, he thought. The attraction was there, constantly simmering below the surface. He could see it in her eyes, the interest and the wariness. He could sense it in her parted lips. He closed his eyes and deepened the kiss with deliberate languor, his tongue sliding along hers.

Alex writhed beneath him as waves of desire moved through her with each caress of his tongue. She buried her fingers in his thick hair and whispered his name in a rush of pleasure. Passion began to throb deep inside her, and that jolted her back to reality. Enough, she mentally shouted, he's not interested in marrying you. Don't get involved. She opened her eyes in the middle of the kiss and sighed.

"I don't like the sound of that sigh," Casey murmured.

"It was a great kiss, but I'm afraid it's over."

Man, this was going to be tough. The woman had willpower. He felt her yielding to him, felt the heat of her response, and then the door closed and she was gone—off on a husband hunt. What a bummer. Casey, he silently asked himself, how could a smart guy like you get yourself into such a mess? He pushed away from her and stood. "I suppose you want your ice cream now?"

"Yup." She kept her gaze steady, not wanting to reveal her true feelings. She'd already shown more than she should have. Casey was getting to her. She hadn't wanted to stop kissing him. He stoked a need in her that was hard to deny. And she liked him, that was the awful part. She could handle a physical attraction, but she was finding it more and more difficult to ignore the combination of emotions he aroused in her. She'd come to Alaska to find a nice dull husband, but her mind was becoming cluttered with Casey. If she wasn't careful, she'd fall in love with him, and where would that leave her? Heartbroken and lonely and dissatisfied.

Alex dressed quickly while Casey shuffled around in the kitchen. She was tired and her muscles ached, but she forced herself to pull on her jeans and a sweatshirt. She swung her backpack onto her shoulder and joined Casey. The luxury of a soft bed was tempting, but it wouldn't be smart to stay here tonight. The less she saw of Casey, the better off she'd be.

Casey wasn't surprised when he saw her. If he were in her position, he'd turn tail and run too. And because he was in his position, he taunted her. He handed her a dish of chocolate ice cream, leaned against the counter and lazily crossed his arms over his chest. "Leaving?"

Alex let ice cream melt on her tongue before answering. "Mmmm. I think it's best if I sleep in the tent tonight."

"My bed is big and comfortable and warm. You're going to regret leaving it."

His posture was casual but there was an air of restrained energy about him. He reminded Alex of a cat hunting a mouse. He was waiting, he was amused by the chase, and he was anticipating success. Without realizing it, he'd issued a challenge to her. This was war, and Alex had no intention of losing.

Five

It was just past dawn when Alex crawled from her
sleeping bag, inhaling cold air smelling of damp
earth, alpine moss and the hardy grasses that
filled her property. Trees stood sentinel straight;
no breeze disturbed them. Small birds chirrupped
nearby, impatiently waiting for the sun to warm
them. Alex pulled her cashmere sweater over her
T-shirt and gratefully put on the heavy wool shirt
Casey had insisted she buy. Bruno heaved himself to his feet, looked at the world through bleary
rottweiler eyes, and reluctantly plodded outdoors
with Alex. The world seemed to stretch limitless
in front of the woman and the dog, a sweeping
vista of gray-green bog and pastel-colored hills.
The barely discernible snowcapped peaks of the
Alaska Range seemed to melt into the pearly morning sky.

Alex turned her attention to the hillside behind her. Not far away, Casey was brewing coffee. She could feel his presence in her aching bones. She had no intention of falling prey to his alluring bed, but a hot shower, a flush toilet, fresh ground coffee and a toasted muffin were temptations she couldn't resist. She trudged toward the path to his house, acknowledging that she was a weak woman.

A fragrant curl of smoke assured her Casey was up and had a fire going to dispel the morning chill. No doubt he was waiting for her with that maddening, self-satisfied smile playing at the corners of his mouth. She rapped on the sliding patio door and waved to Casey, who was pouring coffee into a Styrofoam cup.

"I ran out of dishes," he explained when he opened the door.

"Why don't you wash the dirty ones?"

"I keep forgetting." He took a frozen bagel from the freezer and dropped it into a paper bag while he sipped the hot liquid. "I didn't expect to see you up so early."

Alex wasn't sure if she ever got to sleep. This wilderness stuff took some getting used to. She needed noise, even a few eighteen wheelers in the distance. She needed a warm nose to breathe through, real sheets, an extra firm mattress. She didn't think she'd ever get used to a sleeping bag. And then there were those thoughts about Casey that had her overheating when the temperature had to be dipping into the thirties. Thank goodness she'd be able to move into her cabin today, and tonight she could sleep in her cozy loft bed. She didn't want to explain any of this to Casey, so she shrugged and looked longingly at the coffeepot. "I know I'm being a pest, but I was wondering if I could use your bathroom?"

"You're not a pest, and of course, you can use the bathroom. Unfortunately, I'm in a rush. One of my pilots is sick with the flu, and I'm going to have to do his cargo run today."

"What are you doing with the frozen bagel?"

Casey slipped a down vest over his plaid flannel shirt and pocketed a set of keys from the kitchen counter. "Breakfast. I'll microwave it when I get to the office." He glanced at his watch. "I'm late. Is there anything I can do for you before I take off?"

"Yes. I've decided to work on my cabin today and clean the store tomorrow. Could you get word to Andy? And how do I go about getting my own bathroom?"

"Are you talking indoor plumbing?"

Alex sighed. "No. I'm talking cheap."

Casey looked at her soberly, wishing she had a little less pluck. He hated seeing her making an emotional and financial investment that was doomed. He contemplated another attempt to explain the realities of an Alaskan winter, but decided against it. He knew she wouldn't listen, she was determined to find out for herself. "I'll make arrangements for someone to come around and build you an outhouse." He grabbed his bagel and coffee and paused at the door. "There's an extra set of keys on my dresser. I'm driving the Bronco. That leaves the truck for you in case you need it. Make yourself at home."

A nice sentiment, she thought, but this wasn't a home. It was a garbage dump, a health hazard. She was desperate for a cup of coffee, but she wasn't going to drink it out of a Styrofoam cup or out of a mug that should have been labeled "Mold experiment in progress." She loaded the dishwasher and began working her way through the kitchen, organizing cupboards, scouring utensils, shining appliances. She gathered trash from the living room, filling three trash bags, and moved on to the bedroom. By noon the house was sparkling clean. Alex set a bowl of freshly cut flowers on the polished surface of the round oak table and stepped back to survey her labors. It looked nice, it smelled nice, and she didn't have to worry about getting typhoid from the coffee.

"Okay, Bruno," she said, "now it's time to work on *our* house." She took the keys to the truck and went out to the garage where Casey had stored her furniture and household goods. It took her an hour to load everything into the truck. She opened the passenger door and shoved the sullen rottweiler onto the bench seat. "Bruno, you're just not into the spirit of this. We're Alaskans now. We have to get out there and tote that barge and lift that bale. It'll be good for you," she said, sliding behind the wheel. "You need to get some exercise. You need to lose some of that blubber."

She drove carefully down the winding hill, and

the truck bounced along the ruts and hillocks of her driveway. She backed the truck as close to her front door as possible and began moving her possessions into the cabin. Even with the windows open and spotlessly clean, the interior of the little hut wasn't nearly as light as Casey's log house. The inside of the cabin had darkened over the years, absorbing smoke from the iron stove, while aromas of sourdough and fried bacon had permeated the thick log walls.

Alex took a screwdriver from her hip pocket and attached new curtain rods to the window frames. When the rods were secure, she hung the white ruffled curtains and tied them back to admit as much sunshine as possible. She dragged the double-size mattress to the clean loft, made her bed up with white sheets and pillowcases trimmed in eyelet and topped it with the cherry-red down comforter. She covered a small square table with a red and white checkered tablecloth and set a hurricane lamp in the middle. Tomorrow she would go into town and get kerosene for it. A list began forming in her mind. She needed to go to the supermarket for food, she should check at the post office to see if her cartons of clothes had arrived, she had to open a checking account, and she should begin cleaning the store.

Alex arranged two ladder-back chairs at her table and carted a small chest of drawers into the cabin, placing it near the ladder leading to the loft. She'd bought an oval, wood-framed mirror to hand directly over the chest, but decided to hang it another day. There were the details of daily living that had to be attended to before the light faded—makeup arranged on the dresser, shoes tidily lined in the closet, silverware and assorted utensils placed in colorful mugs set on a shelf by the stove. She'd bought a set of dishes and four glasses and now realized she had no way of washing them. Add that to the list—a large dishpan and an even larger pot to heat water. When the carpenter came to build her outhouse, she'd have him build a counter next to the stove. She needed a place to do dishes and prepare food.

She looked around and liked what she saw. It was cozy. Not exactly luxurious living, but that was okay. She'd had lots of years of luxurious living. This would be a year to test herself and see what was deep inside, to find out if she could be Alexandra Scott, wilderness woman. She glanced at the expensive array of cosmetics on her dresser, and thought about the clothes en route from New Jersey. There were several boxes of winter things —a down jacket, heavy ski sweaters, knit hats and fur lined gloves. There were also suits, party dresses, satin nighties and silk shirts. What on earth was she going to do with all those dress-for-success clothes? She tipped her head back and laughed out loud. She'd be the only woman in Alaska who chopped wood in $95 lizard slingbacks.

It was five-thirty when Casey pulled into his garage. He noticed the absence of Alex's furniture and felt a stab of emotion he was reluctant to identify. He was crazy, he told himself. He couldn't resent a woman moving her own possessions out of his garage. She wasn't his wife. Not even his girlfriend. He slammed the door to the Bronco and rolled his eyes in self-disgust. He was over the edge. This was a simple physical attraction, he reminded himself, not to be blown out of proportion.

Casey pushed through the front door and came to an abrupt halt when he saw the flowers on his dining room table. "Oh hell, she's cleaned the house," he muttered, annoyed because he was pleased. His nose twitched. What did he smell? Spaghetti sauce cooking on the stove and garlic bread baking in the oven. She was playing dirty. Clean house, Italian dinner. He had a brief fantasy of her waiting for him in the bedroom but gave it up as too much to ask for.

He hung his down vest on a peg on the wall and called her name, feeling his breath hitch when she appeared in the hall. She was barefoot, fresh from the shower, her face scrubbed and glowing, her hair hanging loose over her shoulders in big damp ringlets. She wore a pair of pale blue, faded jeans and one of his plaid flannel shirts, rolled to her elbows, unbuttoned halfway down her sternum. He'd seen women in sexy underwear, but he'd never seen anything as provocative as Alex in his big flannel shirt. He heard his heart go thump in his chest and then quiet down when he realized she had no idea what sort of picture she presented.

Alex smiled at Casey and padded to the kitchen to stir the spaghetti sauce. "I hope you don't mind. I used your shower, and I borrowed a shirt. This is my last night of luxury. Tomorrow I'm going to become more independent." She tasted the sauce and added a couple shakes of oregano. "And tomorrow I'm going to do my laundry."

"It was nice of you to clean my house. It looks great."

"It was only fair. You helped me with my cabin." She pulled the garlic bread out of the oven and slid it onto a breadboard. "I took the liberty of making us supper. I thought we could discuss the store while we ate."

Casey put two place mats on the table, then plates and silverware. "So this is a business dinner," he said, standing behind Alex while she rinsed the spaghetti, running his finger down her back in a casual exploration that told him she was braless. "For a minute there, I thought you were trying to seduce me with a romantic meal."

Alex plopped the pasta into a large bowl. "You were wrong," she said flatly. "If I was going to seduce you, I wouldn't have made garlic bread." Her eyes dropped to her unbuttoned shirt, and she realized she should have buttoned one more button. Too late now. If she fidgeted with the shirt, she would only draw attention to it. She'd just keep the conversation impersonal and hope for the best. Last night she'd been tired and not up to defending her virtue. Tonight would be different. Just let him try something. Tonight she was ready with the answers.

Casey sat next to her at the table and speared a tomato wedge from his salad bowl. "What's to discuss about the store?"

Alex sprinkled Parmesan on her spaghetti. "I thought I would start cleaning it up tomorrow. It needs some electrical work, light fixtures and painting." She ticked the items off on her fingers. "It needs a name, I want to start thinking about future inventory, and I need to make arrangements for insurance."

Casey grinned at her. "You're really excited about this."

"Of course I'm excited. Wouldn't you be excited if you were beginning a new life?"

"Sure. It's just that you're so damn cute when you're excited."

"Cute?"

"Yeah. Your eyes get big and sparkling, and your voice goes up an octave. Cute."

Alex didn't know if she liked being cute. Shirley Temple was cute. Bob Newhart was cute. Her self-image ran more toward Meryl Streep with a lot of hair. She arranged her napkin and started over. "About the name."

Casey studied the graceful slope of her shoulder and the swell of her breasts under the flannel shirt. She was beautiful and intensely feminine, her femininity accentuated by the large masculine shirt, his shirt. It seemed very intimate to him that his shirt was lying against her bare breasts. He realized Alex was watching him, waiting for an answer. "The name. How about Alex and Andy's Sporting Goods?" He knew that would get a rise out of her.

Alex wrinkled her nose.

Casey tipped back in his chair and thought for a minute. "It should be something Alaskan. How about Frontier?"

Alex let it roll through her mind. Frontier. She liked it. "Okay, it'll be Frontier."

Casey got a pad and pencil from a kitchen drawer and set it beside his plate. "I have to fly again tomorrow, but there are some things I can handle from the office before I take off. You concentrate on cleaning, and if you want, I'll hire the electrician and painter. Let's start a list, so I don't forget anything."

The sun was setting when Alex collected the empty plates and carried them to the kitchen. She watched Casey make a few final notations on the pad and felt affection mingle with more earthy emotions. She definitely was falling in love with him. Wasn't that the pits? She liked wearing his shirt, and she liked sitting across from him at the dinner table. She even liked the way he looked at her with smoldering, questioning eyes. A good marriage must feel like this, she thought. Comfortable sharing, silences pregnant with love, desire. The urge to reach out to him was so strong, she was afraid to leave the kitchen, so she turned to the sink and busied herself rinsing plates and glasses. Don't lose sight of reality, she told herself. He's not interested in marriage. Remember last night when you left, determined to win the battle of the dueling libidos? Alex smiled. What she remembered about last night was how endearing he was when he bargained for a kiss with a dish of ice cream.

Casey brought the remaining dishes from the table to the kitchen counter. He noticed the determined set of Alex's shoulders as she scrubbed imaginary spots from clean plates, and he wondered about her mood. Hard to believe she hadn't felt the intimacy between them as they'd made plans about the store and shared a meal. The air had been so thick with suppressed desire he could hardly breathe. He lightly caressed her shoulder and let his hand trail the length of her arm and settle at her waist. "You look like a woman with a lot on her mind."

Alex stood very still, absorbing the pleasure of his touch, afraid to respond but wanting him to continue.

Casey hadn't expected an answer to his question. He could see the pulse fluttering in her neck and knew she was victim to the same fierce attraction he was experiencing. His hand molded to her hip, his thumb extending above the waistband of her jeans, rubbing across the soft flannel shirt. Her hair was thick and sweet, inviting him to tangle his fingers in its silky lushness, to lift the heavy fall and kiss the hidden nape of her neck. He felt the tension coiling in his gut and

took a deep breath, wanting desperately to remove the shirt and press himself against her bare
back, to feel the weight of her breasts in his hands.
He closed his eyes and strained toward her, wrapping her in his arms, burying his face in her dark
hair. He wanted to share his passion with her, tell
her about the erotic dreams she'd inspired, seduce her with the exotic, sensual images flooding
his brain, but his tongue felt thick and his throat
was raw with desire. He spun her around and
took her mouth hungrily, feeling feverish with
need, knowing he was soon going to be beyond
reason, beyond control. He ran his hands under
her shirt to cup her full breasts, gasping as the
hard nub of her nipple burned into his palm. No
woman should have such power over a man, he
thought somberly, feeling lost to his violent need.

Alex sensed her power and acquiesced. A yearning had swept over her so quickly and so completely that she hadn't even attempted to fight it,
acknowledging that they were already mentally
and emotionally joined. The physical joining seemed
so inevitable, she couldn't imagine it not happening. Their tongues met as Alex pulled at his shirt
until it was free of his jeans, and she could feel
his heated skin beneath her hand. They looked
into each other's eyes, and a silent communica-
tion passed between them, a mutual affirmation
that quickened Alex's heartbeat and caused her
grip to tighten on his waist. Casey parted her
shirt, exposing her breasts, and slowly drew his
fingertip over an aroused nipple. He rolled the

rosy nub between his thumb and forefinger and teased it with the tip of his tongue, as Alex gasped with the fiery thrill of pleasure. Heat roiled through her stomach and pulsed against the confining material of her jeans. She felt swollen, heavy with wanting, desperate for him to ease the delicious, insistent, unrelenting tension of desire that was enslaving her.

They moved to the bedroom and let passion guide them as they undressed each other in an act of sexual exploration. The sheets were cool and the room dusky when he moved over her, flesh against flesh. Alex watched Casey with heavy lidded eyes, knowing he wasn't exactly what she'd come to Alaska looking for, but satisfied that he was everything she'd hoped to find. He was the adventure, the missing piece in her life that money and power couldn't buy, and she gave herself up to him, guiding him to secret fantasies she'd never before shared. She felt herself approaching the pinnacle of pleasure and opened her legs to him, panting against the heat of his marauding mouth as he kissed her to the point of no return before losing control and plunging himself into her, riding the waves of her release to achieve his own.

Casey shifted his weight but made no move to leave her. They lay together, bodies entwined, silently thinking private thoughts, contemplating what had just happened. When Alex shivered involuntarily, Casey pulled the quilt over them, carefully tucking it around her shoulders before drawing her back to him.

Alex had known a few men, but she'd never experienced anything like this. In the quiet aftermath, she felt frightened by the intensity of their lovemaking. She'd given everything and taken everything and now she wasn't sure what she had left. She wasn't a woman who lied to herself, and she didn't do so now. She was desperately in love with Casey despite her desire not to be.

Casey held Alex close, stroking her glossy curls long after she had fallen asleep, deriding himself for letting this happen. He'd fallen in love with a woman who thought bears were cuddly, a New York career girl off on a lark to catch a husband. Exactly what he didn't need. He should have had the sense to keep his hands to himself, but no, he had to give in to his urges. Now what? How do you walk away from something like this? Dammit, Casey, he thought, haven't you made enough mistakes? Don't you ever learn? He watched the digital clock change minutes to hours, not wanting to sleep away this time he had with Alex. There wouldn't be many more nights like this. Tomorrow he was going to find her a husband, and it wasn't going to be him.

Alex heard the shower running and squinted into the darkness at the bedside clock. Five-thirty. Memories of the preceding night flooded through her, along with the fact that Casey had to fly this morning. She reluctantly crawled from the warm bed, slipped Casey's shirt over her naked body, and languorously walked to the kitchen, enjoying the warmth of his modern house, thinking she'd never before fully appreciated central heating. She made coffee and slid a perfectly browned omelet onto a plate just as Casey appeared in the kitchen. She took a cinnamon roll from the microwave and placed it next to the omelet.

Casey lounged against the counter, watching her assemble his breakfast. She was wearing his shirt again and had buttoned exactly three buttons. When she raised her arms to get a coffee mug from an overhead cabinet, a tantalizing sight showed beneath the tail of the shirt. And when she turned, a perfect triangle of black curls beckoned to him for just a second before the shirt swung back into place. He took the plate from her and choked back a wave of desire so strong, it made his hand shake. He kept his eyes on the omelet, eating quickly. He had to get out of there fast, he thought, before he was back in bed, begging her to marry him.

He poured his coffee into a spill-proof mug and went in search of his keys and jacket. "I'm in a hurry," he said gruffly. "I'll take the coffee with me." He gave her a perfunctory peck on the cheek and turned to leave. "I'll send the carpenters to your cabin this morning. Make sure you're waiting for them," he called over his shoulder in a voice that sounded grimly strained.

She was at her cabin by seven-thirty, and at nine a pickup rumbled and bounced along her driveway, coming to a stop just a few feet from her front door. A second truck appeared and parked beside the first. A mountain of a man with long brown hair and a closely cropped beard ambled over to Alex. "You the lady that needs an outhouse?"

"Yes, I'm afraid I am."

"Casey sent us. He said he gave me and my brother the job 'cause we have brown hair. And he says to tell you we aren't married. I don't know what that means, but here we are."

The guileless statement took Alex by surprise. Casey was sending her prospective bridegrooms. A stab of pain sliced through her heart, immediately followed by black rage. He'd gotten what he'd wanted, and now he was dumping her, foisting her off on a carpenter. Michael Casey was fungus, pond slime. He thought he could buy her a toilet seat and make her fall in love with him, and then get himself off the hook by sending her a brown-haired latrine builder. Alex pressed her lips together and made an effort at self-control. Maybe this was supposed to be a joke. Casey couldn't be this insensitive, this cruel. She was getting upset over nothing. Where was her sense of humor? She rolled her eyes and gave the bewildered carpenter an embarrassed smile. "Do you know much about outhouses?" she asked him.

"Everything there is to know."

"Good, because I don't know anything about them. Put it wherever it's supposed to go, and make it look like whatever it's supposed to look like. I have to go into town. I don't suppose you need me for anything?"

"Don't suppose we do. We'll leave the bill tacked to your front door."

Alex got her purse and, she and Bruno plodded up the hill to Casey's house. She'd have to take his truck because she couldn't fit cleaning equipment in her car. She hefted the dog onto the seat and pressed her lips together at the churning in her stomach. It no longer felt comfortable to use Casey's truck. She wanted to think the carpenter had been a joke, but she wasn't sure. If it had been a joke, it was in bad taste. Either way, she wasn't pleased with Casey.

She was struggling with the heavy front door of the store when an electrician's truck pulled into the rutted parking lot. The man was long faced and lean with brown hair pulled into a ponytail. He approached Alex and offered to help with the door. "You the lady who needs an electrician?" he added.

She grimly looked at his hair and nodded her head.

The man gave the door a yank and swung it open for Alex to pass. "Casey sent me," he said with a wide smile. "He says you're looking for an electrician and a husband, is that true?"

"What else did Casey say?"

The young man squinted at the overhead wiring. "He didn't say much else. He said I should just come look you over and make up my own mind."

Alex picked up a three-pound Hudson Bay cruising ax that had been left lying on the counter and thought of its possible uses on men. "Make sure the wiring is safe and up-to-date. I want baseboard sockets and at least two more overhead fixtures. Unfortunately, I don't have the fixtures yet."

"That's okay. I can come back for that. You want to go to the movies tonight?"

Alex gripped the ax a little tighter. "You want to live to see tomorrow?"

"Honey, you're never gonna get married with an attitude like that." He shook his head. "No wonder Casey has to help you out."

Thumb screws were too good for Michael Casey, Alex decided. She was going to make him pay for this. This was too much.

Late in the afternoon Alex passed her little red car parked at the entrance to her driveway and regarded it sadly. It had been such a source of pride and enjoyment in New Jersey, and now it sat in dusty rejection like some forsaken orphan. "That's pitiful," she said to Bruno. "Just look at that poor car, out there all by itself." She continued up the driveway, holding tightly to the wheel as the truck bounced toward her cabin. "We need stones, about fourteen zillion tons of them. Then this will be a real road, and I can park my little car right next to my front door." Bruno clenched his teeth and braced himself for the ruts made by the carpenters' trucks.

Her new outhouse stood downwind of the cabin,

partially hidden by a copse of freshly transplanted spruce saplings. "Bruno, look at it! It's my outhouse. My very own outhouse." Alex ran to the small wooden structure. She tipped her head back and laughed at the half-moon painted on the door. Who would believe it? Certainly no one back in Princeton. The wood had been stained and varnished to match the cabin, and a wet paint sign dangled from a shiny brass doorknob. Alex carefully peeked inside. It was roomier than she'd expected with a small shelf built into one wall. She looked up at a bubbletop skylight. A yuppie outhouse if she ever saw one.

Casey sauntered across the field. Hell hath no fury like a woman scorned, he thought to himself as he kept a cautious distance from Alex. "Nice outhouse," he said.

Alex turned slowly to face him. She felt the anger burning in her eyes, but she kept her expression calm. She wasn't going to give him the satisfaction of provoking her. Two could play this game. "Thanks to your brown-haired carpenters."

"Just trying to be helpful."

"Mmmm," Alex murmured, walking back to her cabin. "It was very thoughtful of you, but they weren't my type. Too big. And the electrician was very nice, but I'm not partial to ponytails."

Casey followed a few steps behind, suspicious of the affable tone of her voice. "Maybe it would help if you told me exactly what you were looking for."

"About six foot," Alex said, moving toward the

truck, "broad shoulders, flat stomach and a really great butt." She took a box from the back of the pickup and flashed him a flat look. "You know, good breeding stock."

Casey breathed an audible sigh of relief to find he hadn't been wrong in his assessment of the female mind. She was madder than hell. She just wasn't going to demean herself by showing it. And she had a wicked sense of humor. He grabbed a box and a grocery bag and followed her into the house. "Looks like you've been shopping."

"I left the store early to stop by the post office and get some of the stuff I shipped from New Jersey. I think I'm only missing one carton. And I stopped at the supermarket and bought healthy food. No doughnuts."

"How will Bruno survive without doughnuts?"

"It's going to be tough. We'll probably both go into withdrawal."

Casey stacked cans of fruit and jars of juice on the shelves next to the cookstove. He lined up boxes of cereal and noodles. He stepped back to admire the colorful arrangement.

"That's a work of art," Alex told him. "You have a definite flair with cereal."

"This whole cabin is a work of art. I think I like it better than my house."

"Want to trade?"

Casey grinned. "Can't wait to get your hands on my plumbing, huh?"

Alex bit her tongue at the double entendre. Mr. Love 'Em and Leave 'Em would blanch if he knew that she'd like to make sure he never plumbed again. She opened a large cardboard box and hastily transferred the silky contents to her chest of drawers. "Okay, that's it," she said. "Thanks for your help." They walked outside, and she realized she'd have to drive his truck back to his house. "I'll follow you in the truck."

Casey nodded and slid behind the wheel. He was doing it again, he thought grimly. He was flirting with her. And when he got her up to the house, he knew he'd try to seduce her. He was being honest with himself. His good intentions weren't worth a damn when he got within touching range of Alexandra Scott. The woman was a menace. He drove the Bronco into the garage and went directly to the house, forcing her to bring the keys to him.

Alex felt the anger rising in waves clear up to the roots of her hair when she realized what he was doing. She stood on the threshold of the patio door and dangled his keys from her fingertip.

"You're probably hungry," Casey said. "Would you like to split a can of soup with me?"

"No. I have to go home and get a good night's sleep. You never know what tomorrow will bring. Maybe Prince Charming. Have you picked out my sign painter yet?"

"I had someone in mind, but he doesn't have a really great butt. I'll have to go back through my little black book."

They stood for several seconds, sizing each other up, each smiling a tight smile that didn't quite reach to their eyes. "Will you be up for breakfast?" Casey asked in a lazy drawl.

"No."

"How about a shower?" He knew he was pushing it, but he couldn't resist. She was fun to tease.

She rolled her eyes and turned to leave.

"Wait. You can't go yet. I have your toilet seat."

"How could I have forgotten."

Casey retrieved a box from the closet and tucked it under Alex's arm. "And you'll need this." A roll of toilet paper. "Okay, you can go now."

Alex gave an exasperated sigh and moved away from the door.

"Hold it," Casey said, snagging her by the elbow. "One more thing."

"Now what?"

Strong, warm hands brushed gently along the planes of her face and tangled in her hair, cradling her head. His lips were soft and coaxing, and his tongue penetrated her mouth and withdrew reluctantly. "Good night."

Alex opened her mouth to speak, but she was so furious and so aroused that no words came out. She narrowed her eyes, turned on her heel and strode across his lawn.

Six

Alex was reluctant to leave the comfort of her big down quilt, looking at the geometric patterns of sunlight on her freshly varnished floor. But Bruno sat by the door, waiting for her to get up and let him out, so she pushed the hair out of her eyes and crawled to the ladder. She sucked in her breath when her bare feet hit the frigid floor and cold air swirled up her loose-fitting nightgown. She quickly pulled on the bottoms to the long johns Casey had persuaded her to buy, and a pair of red woolen socks. Just for good measure, she laced up her brand new, heavy-duty hiking boots. Snapping shut a blue and red ski parka over her pink, mid-calf nightie, she flung the front door open and said, "Okay, Bruno, go do whatever it is Alaskan dogs do." She opened her eyes wide and gasped at the sight of Casey standing just inches from her, hand poised in midair, ready to knock on her door.

"Morning," Casey drawled.

"You scared the daylights out of me!"

Casey looked her over. "You're pretty scary too. You look like Mammy Yokum. Is this a new approach to birth control?"

"I'm freezing to death!"

"Honey, it's only the beginning of September. It's thirty-five degrees. That's balmy by Alaskan standards," he said, making no move to step inside.

Alex twitched her nose and sniffed the air. "I smell coffee."

A plastic laundry basket sat on the ground at Casey's feet. He pointed to it. "I brought you a thermos."

Alex noticed it was leaning against a stack of clothes that had been freshly washed and neatly folded. "You did my laundry?"

"Yeah. This is the first time I've ever had fun doing the laundry. I especially like the black lace panties with the little red bows."

"This is embarrassing."

"I'm on my way to work. Anything you'd like me to do for you, besides sending over a sign painter?"

"I'd like to have a phone installed at the store."

Casey nodded. "How about your driveway? You want to have it done before the first snow falls and the ground gets too hard to level."

"Try to get me a low price."

Casey played with the tag on her jacket zipper.

"Hey, those guys with the great butts don't come cheap. You get what you pay for."

Alex nodded her head in mute agreement. She clutched her jacket to her throat and wondered if there really was a God. And did He have a bizarre sense of humor? Was He getting a chuckle out of pitting her against Michael Casey? She took the laundry basket, mumbled "thank you," and hastily retreated back inside her cabin.

In the past two weeks Alex had seen only three customers, and they hadn't bought anything. She listened to rain drumming on the tin and tar paper roof and prowled the showroom like a caged animal. The store was now scrubbed and freshly painted. New overhead lighting had been installed and a coffeepot perked on a sideboard in an attempt to dispel the gloom pervading the coarse room.

Andy poked his head out of his private den and ambled to the coffeepot. "Run out of things to do?" he inquired. "Don't ya want to scrub something one more time?"

Alex gave him a murderous look that warned him sarcasm wasn't appreciated.

"Women," he mumbled, filling his cup and returning to the back room.

The front door swung open and Casey came in dragging a carton behind him. He'd seen Alex only briefly since he'd done her laundry and brought her a thermos of coffee. The theory had been since he couldn't control himself when he was near her, he'd stay far away, but her very presence on his mountain ate away at him. Every evening he walked through the woods to the perimeter of her property to be sure she was safe. He would stand for a moment, staring at the golden light pouring from the cabin window and watch for the familiar feminine shadow to move into his line of vision. Every morning he would drive by the store to be sure her car was parked in the lot. For the past three days he'd been in San Francisco securing a new freight contract and had pacified his loneliness by shopping for presents. He looked around the room and smiled his approval to Alex. "It's nice. Much brighter. Smells better."

Alex felt her heart jump at the sight of him. He looked ruggedly handsome in a black and red plaid wool jacket, black jeans and hiking boots. Raindrops clung to strawberry-blond hair that was in need of a cut, and a broad, slightly embarrassed smile creased his face and lit his enigmatic hazel eyes. She'd passed him on the driveway twice, and he'd briefly stopped in the store while she was cleaning, but that had been it. She'd assumed the sight of her in long johns and nightgown had been sufficient to squash all romantic interests.

Casey moved to the counter. "Coffee?" He rapped his knuckles against the glass canister of chocolate chip cookies. "Cookies?"

"For the customers. Except there aren't any."

Casey took a cookie. "Business is bad?"

"Business is nonexistent."

"It'll perk up." He ate the cookie leisurely and stared at her, feeling the magnetic pull of her personality, feeling the pleasant flush of desire wash over him. "How's Andy?"

Alex smiled. "He's not so bad. He's like a porcupine, all bristly on the topside with a soft belly on the underside."

Casey continued to stare at her. "What about the guy with the great butt? Has he been around?"

Alex tried not to laugh. "The sign painter wasn't bad from behind, but he had an IQ that was smaller than his shoe size."

"This husband-hunting stuff is pretty rough, huh?"

Alex shrugged. "It'll perk up."

A muscle twitched in Casey's jaw, but his expression remained impassive. The door opened, and a man entered on a gust of cold air. "I'm new here," he said. "Those gas pumps work?"

Casey leaned forward and whispered in Alex's ear, touching the sensitive shell with his lips as he spoke, "Brown hair."

Alex glared at him. "Don't start."

Casey pointedly ignored her and approached the man with congenial interest. "Married?"

"No."

Casey beamed. "He's not married."

Alex pressed her lips together.

"Well, what do you think? He's got brown hair. Would you like to marry him?"

The man looked uncomfortable.

"Alex came to Alaska to find a husband," Casey
explained. "He has to have brown hair."

The man put his hand to his head. "I have
brown hair."

"Are you rich?"

"No."

"You see," he told Alex, "he's perfect."

Alex grit her teeth and threw a coffee cup a
Casey. He deftly caught it with one hand. "She's
been having a hard time landing someone on her
own," Casey confided, "so I've been helping her."

Alex hurled two chocolate chip cookies at him.
He caught one, but the other bounced off his
forehead. "See how much fun she is, never a dull
moment. What do you say? Wanna be a sport and
marry her?"

"She looks a little violent."

"I like to think she's just high-spirited."

The man grinned and shook his head. "I think
you have your work cut out for you," he told Casey.
"About the gas pumps?"

"They don't work," Alex answered, sending a
bloodcurdling sidelong glance at Casey.

Casey walked the man outside and directed him
to a gas station farther down the road. He was
practically bursting with good humor when he
came back in.

Alex had her fists clenched. "You humiliated
me!"

"Just trying to be helpful."

"You weren't trying to be helpful. You were trying

to prove a point. You were trying to make me look ridiculous."

Casey wagged a finger at her. "Not true. I realized right from the start that you were too shy and retiring. You definitely need help." He leaned across the counter and drew a lazy line on her chin. "I'm prepared to help you however I can. I'll even let you practice, um, mating techniques on me."

"I'd like to practice using my carving knife on you."

"All that will change when you see what I brought you."

Alex looked at the carton. "Is that it?"

"No. That's just a box of shotgun shells I picked up for Andy. Your present's in the truck."

"You really shouldn't be bringing me presents. You already gave me a toilet seat."

Casey propped the front door open with a keg of nails. "This is different. This is for the store. It's an old Alaskan custom."

"Uh-huh."

He went to his truck, pulled out a huge tarpaulin-wrapped form, and wheeled it in on a hand truck. "I saw this and immediately thought of you. I couldn't resist it."

Alex's eyes got wide. Whatever it was, it was big. Over seven feet tall. It was almost to the ceiling.

Casey carefully unwrapped the tarp and with a grand flourish revealed a stuffed grizzly. The big bear was poised on his hind feet, arms at his sides, a piercing expression in his beady bear eyes, mouth slightly parted. A masterpiece of modern taxidermy, it seemed to be asking directions to the nearest bar.

Alex didn't know what to say. It was horrible. The moosehead over the cash register was bad enough, but the bear . . . The bear was beyond words.

Casey pushed it into position by the front door. "I think that's the perfect place for it. What do you think?"

"Um . . ."

"I knew you'd be speechless. Is it worth a kiss?"

"No more kisses."

"You don't mean it."

"I do!"

Casey grabbed her in a hug and nuzzled her neck. "Guess I'll just have to take my kisses by force, you uncooperative wench."

"You brute. Get away from me, or I'll sic my dog on you."

"Bruno only attacks people who are carrying concealed doughnuts."

Alex felt her heart skip a beat as Casey pinned her to the wall in a parody of macho dominance. His hard thigh erotically parted her legs.

"This is how that old grizzly'd do it to his mate," Casey said, his voice husky and intimate.

Alex felt her breasts swelling against him and tried to keep her breathing from sounding labored. "But you're not a grizzly, and I'm not your mate."

Casey's eyes dropped to her mouth. It was soft and inviting and filled him with desire.

"Just exactly what am I, Casey?" She was afraid she was simply an amusement, a frivolous toy, a challenge.

He rested his forehead against hers. "Damned if I know, but you're driving me crazy. I was just starting to get my life in order, and then you came along. These past two weeks have been murder. I've missed you every minute of every day."

Alex looked into his eyes and felt her stomach tumble at what she found there. Affection, frustration, longing. She couldn't find a trace of casual emotion. "Why have you been sending me suitors?"

"Because you scare the hell out of me. I'm thinking thoughts no confirmed bachelor has a right to think."

There was a touch of pain in his voice, Alex thought, and a good-sized chunk of honest vulnerability. She saw the beginnings of a smile twitch at the corners of his mouth and knew he was laughing at himself. He was feeling doomed, and she was feeling forgiving and loving. She looped her arms around his neck and kissed him. "I've missed you too." She tipped her head back and laughed at the look of surprise in his eyes.

"What about no more kisses?"

"Ah, the hell with it."

Casey chuckled deep in his throat. He stared at her in wonderment for a moment and drew her to him, claiming her mouth in a kiss that was slow and thoughtful. "Kisses lead to other things, you know."

"Mmmmmmmmm."

His lips recaptured hers, his mouth becoming more demanding, the thrust of his tongue sending shivers of desire racing through her.

"Geez, will you look at this," Andy said, sounding disgusted. "Bad enough I've got a fool woman underfoot all the time, now I have to put up with this smooching stuff. What are the customers gonna think?"

Alex jumped away from Casey and straightened her sweater. "Andy, why is it I never see you unless I'm opening a bag of cookies or doing something embarrassing? Besides, the customers aren't going to think anything. We don't have any customers."

Andy shook his head. "She don't know much, does she?" he said to Casey.

Casey grinned and let his attention turn to the bear. "What do you think, Andy? It's a beauty, huh?"

Andy's eyes sparkled. "Adds a little class to the place."

Casey gathered up the tarp and threw it into the back of his truck. The rain had lessened to a fine mist, and the sun was bright behind a thin blanket of cloud. "I have to get back to the office and do some paperwork," Casey said, pulling Alex onto the front porch and closing the door behind them. "How about if you come up for some grilled salmon steaks tonight?" He drew her to him and nibbled at her lower lip. "And you can be in charge of providing dessert."

Alex stood in line at the Aurora Bakery and cracked her knuckles. She was in charge of dessert. She knew what that meant. The big event. *It.* And that didn't mean pumpkin pie. She took a deep breath and nervously shifted her weight, wondering if she'd made the right decision back in the store. One minute she was saying good riddance to a scoundrel and the next thing she knew, she was agreeing to dinner. It was too sudden, she thought. She'd been seduced by a gross bear and a boyish display of charm.

As an executive she'd prided herself on being an astute judge of character, but she wasn't sure of Casey. There were too many renegade hormones influencing her. Alex, she said to herself, you have to be crazy. What was to guarantee he wouldn't be sending her boyfriends again tomorrow? This was dumb. And on top of everything else, her nails were a mess and she had stubble on her legs. She nodded her head in mute recognition that fate was attempting to step in. She had stubble—that settled it. She certainly wasn't going to make love to Casey when she had stubble.

A woman in a white apron leaned across the counter and looked at Alex. "Can I help you?"

Alex scanned the glass display case. She spoke in a low, confidential voice. "I need something totally decadent."

The woman took a cake from the bottom shelf and slid it onto the counter for Alex's inspection. "Double fudge cake with four gallons of whipped cream icing," she said proudly. "Absolutely orgasmic."

"Perfect. I'll take it." Alex, what are you doing? she silently screamed. You just bought a cake! What about the stubble? She took her wallet from her purse and paid for the cake, thinking Casey wasn't the only one who was doomed.

Half an hour later Alex pulled into Casey's driveway and was relieved to find she'd beaten him home. She put the cake in the refrigerator, threw her backpack onto the bed and headed for the bathroom. She took a fast shower and then spent an inordinately long time brushing her hair into submission, parting it on the side, letting it fall in thick waves and large, soft curls around her face. She added a swipe of mascara to her curly lashes and placed a dab of perfume between her breasts. Looking at herself in the mirror, she was pleased with what she saw. Flat stomach, full breasts, long shapely legs.

She stepped into a pair of lacy white bikini panties and dropped an ivory silk shirtwaist dress over her head. The slick material clung to her, outlining her body's curves, hinting at the dark nipples beneath. The neckline fell in a deep, revealing V, and she took a few steps toward the mirror, critically analyzing the slight sway of her unfettered breasts. Perfect. She smiled, satisfied that she wouldn't come in second best to the orgasmic cake.

Casey saw Alex's red sports car in his driveway and breathed a sigh of relief that she hadn't experienced a change of heart. He hated to admit how much he was looking forward to dinner. After years of happily living alone, he found his house empty. Hell, he thought bitterly, his whole life felt empty without Alex. It was an odd mixture of emotions that was coursing through him. He was in love, and he was angry and disgusted about it.

The sight of Alex in the white dress and strappy little heels intensified his ambiguous feelings. She was stunningly beautiful and totally out of his league. She didn't belong in Alaska. Unfortunately, he thought, none of that stopped him from wanting her. He was mesmerized by the shift of her breasts as she moved around the oak table, laying out flatware for dinner. Desire knotted his stomach and a ripple of fiery heat burned low in his abdomen. He dragged his eyes away from the teasing outline of a dusky, aroused nipple and concentrated on performing the required social amenities. "You look very pretty," he said with a wolfish smile. Despite his misgivings about being in love, he found himself thoroughly enjoying the seductive dress and the promises it made. He set a grocery bag on the counter and took out the salmon steaks and a bottle of wine. He half-filled two stemmed glasses and passed one to Alex. "Any customers yet?"

Alex shook her head, no. "Andy says they'll be coming in tomorrow."

Casey took a box of wooden matches and a bag of charcoal from the broom closet. "Andy should know."

She followed him out to the deck and sipped at her wine. "How does Andy know?"

Casey shrugged. "He knows where the grayling are, and when the salmon will be running. He knows where to pick up a track for the record moose that's been reported outside of Manley. When something comes into season or a rumor starts flying, business gets good because people come to Andy. He was a bush pilot and a guide for years and years. If nobody's catching pike in Minto Flats, they ask Andy about bait." Casey grinned as he lit the fire. "That's when he sells them a new reel and a nine hundred dollar inflatable boat."

"You sound like you're talking from experience."

Casey nodded ruefully. "I've caught some very expensive pike in my time."

After dinner they carried their coffee to the couch and sat side by side watching the fire. Casey slid his arm around her shoulders and nestled her next to him. "Tell me the truth," he said. "What do you think of the bear?"

Alex laughed. "It's awful! But I'm getting used to it, and Andy loves it."

Casey laughed too, a deep and rich rumbling. "I knew you'd hate it, but I couldn't help myself. It's so awful, it's perfect." His eyes grew heavy-lidded and more serious as he traced the slope of her shoulder with his fingertips, enjoying the feel of her, finally allowing himself to ride the wave of loving desire that was sweeping through him. His touch became more firm, his hand applying pressure as passion gripped him. He buried his face in her luxuriant hair and whispered her name. And she turned to him with parted lips that were ready to be kissed.

They went slowly, their lips and tongues grazing lazily along sensitive skin. They were searching out secrets, memorizing lines and planes, drinking in each other's taste. Alex struggled to prolong the loving exploration. She wanted this time to last forever, to remain wrapped in this cocoon of tender passion. She felt him tremble as he moved over her, pressing her into the couch. The tip of his tongue, warm and moist, traced the rim of her ear. His arousal rubbed hard and urgent against her abdomen as hunger surged hot between them, sending flames licking along nerve endings, turning caution and restraint into abandon.

Alex felt his mouth close over her silk clad breast and knew they had skidded to the edge and were out of control. But it was all right because she was with Casey. He raised his head, and she looked into eyes darkened by desire. Listening to his labored breathing, she wondered at the torturous pleasure they could inflict on each other. "Dessert," she whispered thickly.

"No. Not just dessert," he answered. "Much more."

His hands explored the contours of her back and cupped her buttocks as he slowly moved against her in an erotic massage, rubbing his chest against her jutting breasts. A low groan was wrenched from his throat as he kissed her long and deep, his thumb teasing her burning nipple. The skirt to her dress had ridden high, exposing the skimpy lace panties that barely hid her perfect triangle of moist black curls. His hand moved across the lace, tracing tantalizing circles. Then his mouth followed the path of his hand, gentle at first, then driven with the fierce hunger that possessed him.

Alex arched to him in exquisite agony, the need to join fierce in her. She closed her eyes and concentrated on the feel of him, as he sought tender places that were slick with desire. An errant thought flicked through her mind, one brief concern about the wisdom of loving Casey. It was quickly gone, and Alex was lost to the sweetness of his touch.

He shed his clothes and came to her, pulling aside the panty leg to ease himself deep within. She moaned under him, taking him deeper, lifting her hips to his thrusts, cursing the scrap of lace that separated them. She watched him with slitted eyes, panting against his strokes, anticipating the moment.

Casey heard the breath catch in her throat and felt her convulse around him. Sweat beaded on the small of his back as her contractions pulled him forward, stroking him toward his own release. He drove into her, quick and hard, almost instantly pouring his love into her in hot pulses of passion.

When their breathing had returned to normal, Alex looked at her rumpled dress and sighed happily. It had been glorious.

Casey eased himself off her, scooped her into his arms and headed toward the bedroom. "I'm going to deposit you in my big old bed," he said as a smile stole across his face. "I'm hungry for more dessert."

Seven

Casey left the bed and the sleeping woman. He closed the bathroom door to muffle the sound and turned on the shower, hoping the soap and steam could wash away the cold sweat of his nightmare. It had been a long time since he'd awakened in the middle of the night, feeling the overwhelming guilt and aching loneliness. Now it was back. It was back because he was repeating his mistake. "Fool," he cursed himself. He'd made love three times to Alex, the most unlikely woman to ever make an Alaskan wife, and he'd not once used any protection. He let the scorching water pound into his back as if it would pound sense into his head, but when he finally stepped out of the tub, he felt no different than when he'd stepped in. He brushed his teeth, combed his hair, and faced himself squarely in the fogged mirror. He had to make a trip, a long overdue trip. And he was going to make it now.

Alex heard the shower running and glanced at the bedside clock. Four-thirty. She groggily pulled herself to a sitting position as Casey left the bathroom and quickly began to dress. She pushed hair from her eyes and switched on the nightstand lamp. "What are you doing?"

Her voice was husky from sleep and pleasantly amused. It was hard not to love her, Casey thought, hard not to crawl back in bed to her honeyed heat. "I have to leave. I'm flying down to the states. I won't be back for a while. Maybe a week."

Alex felt panic at the terse tone and the clipped answers. Something was wrong, she thought. Last night it had been wonderful, and now everything was feeling precarious. Déjà vu. She dredged a calmness from deep inside and kept her voice even. "Is this business?"

"No. This is personal."

"Want to talk about it?"

"No."

She unconsciously pulled the quilt higher to cover breasts that suddenly felt naked and exposed. The action wasn't lost on Casey. He pressed his lips together and swore softly for hurting her, for making promises he never intended to keep, for leading her on. He wanted to go to her and kiss away the hurt, but he couldn't. He was afraid the kiss would lead to other things, so he angrily slid his feet into a pair of brown penny loafers and threw a handful of essentials into a flight bag. He checked his watch; a plan was forming in his mind. He'd fly his own small jet to L.A. and pick up a commercial flight from there. He slung the flight bag over his shoulder and turned at the door. "I'm sorry."

Alex watched his stiff back retreat into the darkened house, heard him rattling around in the kitchen while he collected keys, and blinked when the front door closed. It was symbolic, she thought. He was walking out of her life. She had never known anything with such certainty or felt the ending of a relationship with such finality. Michael Casey was a complicated man with secrets, and she had no confidence that she could ever breach those secrets. A tear trickled down her cheek. She really did love him, but sometimes love wasn't enough, she realized. All the warning signs had been there, and she'd ignored them. Now what?

She took a shower, washed the sheets, and went home to her little cabin. Then she went back to her stupid store and waited for the guy with brown hair.

Alex felt her eyes glaze over as she peered into the compartmentalized drawer housing several hundred hooks with feathers attached. The man in front of her was angular and lean with the regulation Alaskan beard and thermal underwear showing under the collar of his flannel shirt. He was somewhere in his fifties and was paying for Andy's expertise.

"Okay," he said, sighing in resignation, "I'll take a yellow humpy, a bass duster, and a Dave's red squirrel. I need some leader, forty-pound test." He looked over at Andy and grimaced. "Hell, this'll never come to enough money."

"You know what you need, Dave?" Andy called to him. "You need a new tackle vest. You need one of them dandy rip stop jobs we just got in."

Dave scowled at him. "You didn't just get them in. You got them in last spring, and nobody'd buy 'em."

"Yeah, well maybe so," Andy said, "but you need one of them now."

"Guess I do," Dave agreed, reaching for his wallet.

"Do you still want the yellow duster and the bass humper?" Alex asked.

Dave stared at her blank face for a moment before looking around at Andy. "Bass humper?"

Andy shook his head and rolled his eyes. "She ain't never fished. She just knows about New York stuff."

Dave took a cookie from the cookie jar. "She makes good cookies."

"Hell, she buys 'em," Andy said.

Dave took his vest and change and smiled at Alex. "Well, she buys good cookies," he said on the way out.

Alex slumped against the counter. Maybe this wasn't such a good idea. She couldn't contribute anything to the store but cookies, and they weren't even homemade. They weren't homemade because she couldn't figure out how to work her woodstove. She could make smoke, but she was damned if she could make heat. Casey probably could show her, but she was reluctant to ask. He'd come home late last night after a week's absence and hadn't stopped by to say hello.

Andy made a disgusted sound. "So, you don't know a bass duster when you see one. You can't help it if you're a dumb New York female. Hell, you aren't going to cry, are you?"

"You know much about Casey?"

"As much as anyone, I guess."

"You know where he was last week?"

Andy shrugged. "Outta the state."

"Where out of the state?"

"Butch Miller says he went to see his boy."

Alex stood up a little straighter. "His boy?"

"Yeah, you know. His son."

Her heart felt as if it had stopped. He'd never told her he had a son. He'd never even indicated he'd been married.

"Oh, geez," Andy said, looking at her white face. "He never told you." Andy shook his head. "It's not something he likes to talk about, I suppose. The kid was just a year old when Ellen packed up and left. People tell me she went to Florida."

"Florida? That's so far away."

"Yup. I guess that's why she picked it. The farther, the better. Made it hard on Casey."

Alex ran her hand over the smooth glass countertop. How could you know so much about a person, and still know so little? "I think I'll go home early today."

Andy nodded. "Drive careful."

Casey was on his deck when she drove up. He was sitting on the edge with his feet dangling, staring at the Alaska Range far in the distance. "They look like clouds," he said. "Pristine, unapproachable."

"I'd like to see them up close someday."

"The Range is massive. It begins slowly, not with foothills, but with a steady grade. You'll be driving down the highway, and all of a sudden you'll realize you're above the tree line. Nothing on either side of you but gravel and moss and some rock where the highway's been carved. It's a harsh landscape that doesn't always appeal to tourists."

"As opposed to Florida . . ."

Casey's eyebrows rose slightly in surprise.

Alex sat beside him on the edge of the deck. "Why didn't you tell me?"

"I didn't know what to say. I fathered a kid who calls someone else Dad. I send money. I send presents. Twice a year I take a week off to visit him, but he doesn't know me. He's ten years old. He doesn't know what it all means."

"Your wife remarried?"

"Yup."

"Do you still love her?"

Casey lay back on the deck and laced his hands behind his head. His voice sounded tired. "No. That stopped a long time ago. I'm not sure I ever loved her. I thought I did, but . . ." He closed his eyes. "We were students at Berkeley. She was a golden bronzed California girl, and I was the rugged macho Alaskan. I quit school, said good-bye to Ellen McInerney, and returned to Alaska to make my fortune. She found out she was pregnant. We got married." He waved his hand in a gesture of resignation. "It just was never right. She hated Alaska. I hated everywhere else. She stuck it out for one year after the baby was born, and then left. It wasn't nice."

"You're judging me by her."

"I'm trying to learn by my mistakes. Divorce doesn't bother me. Divorce is something that happens between two consenting adults, but having an absentee son is wrong. I walked that kid through colic, teething, and DPT shots, and then one day he was gone. I'm not going to bring another absentee son into this world."

"We're not even married, and already you're planning our divorce."

"Damn, Alex, Look at you! You've got on a suede skirt and heels. You've never been fishing, never been hunting, never been hiking. You think bears are cuddly. What the hell are you going to do in Alaska for the rest of your life? Maybe if you were in Anchorage . . ." He shook his head. "No, not even in Anchorage. You're a New York executive, you're not going to be happy hanging around here."

"I admit I like wearing pretty clothes. I also like Alaska. I don't see where the two are incompatible. You must think I'm pretty shallow."

"Not at all. I think you're gutsy and intelligent

and aggressive." Casey stood and paced the deck. "This is an adventure right now, but by the end of the winter the adventure will have turned into tedium. I don't think Alaska holds the kind of stimulation you need, and I don't want to find out the hard way, at some innocent kid's expense. I never intended for it to go this far. I'm sorry. It won't work out between us. We're too different."

"Maybe I'll turn out to like fishing."

"You'll hate it. It'll ruin your nails."

Alex jumped up beside him and poked her perfectly manicured finger at his chest. "That does it. Now I'm really steamed. You're nothing but a sexist bigot. Who gave you the right to decide whether or not I'll like fishing?" She poked him again. "You don't deserve me. I'd be better off with the sign painter."

"He'll be drooling and eating gruel after two weeks with you."

"I'm leaving. And I'm not coming back." She started toward her car, then pivoted on her heel. "Oh yeah, one last thing, would you show me how to work my woodstove?"

"Do you have any wood?"

"Would you show me how to chop wood?"

Casey grimaced. "Go change your clothes, and I'll be down in ten minutes."

Hours later Alex extinguished her kerosene lamp and stiffly climbed up to her loft bed. She'd had some success with the stove, but the wood chopping . . . She groaned. She'd emulated Casey's every move, but just couldn't get the hang of it.

She slid under the quilt and closed her eyes. Good thing he wasn't around when she chopped off part of the toe to her hiking boot. Tomorrow would be a better day, she told herself. The chopping would get easier.

She stared at the moonlight spilling through her window and admitted it wasn't the chopping that bothered her. She wasn't bothered by the lack of stimulation that Casey worried about either. She was bothered by the lack of interesting men. She'd imagined them flocking into her hardware store like lemmings making their final, fatal migration. Well, it wasn't like that. Mostly old men came to her store, and the young men were . . . wrong. What was wrong with them? They weren't Casey. She was in love with him and didn't want anyone else. And she didn't ever want to leave Alaska. She loved the size of the land, the feeling of timelessness, and the power of the elements. She pressed her palms against her eyelids. She was tired. Things would look better in the morning.

The little red car hummed along the highway and turned onto the gravel road. Alex looked at the wood stacked on the seat next to her and grinned. What she lacked in hardiness, she more than made up for in sneakiness and resourcefulness. She intended to learn how to chop wood someday. In the meantime, she'd buy it and lie through her teeth. Anyone as bigoted and stubborn as Casey deserved to be hornswoggled. He also deserved to be happily married; that's what she'd decided when she woke up this morning. And she was going to help him reach that blissful state. She was going to convince him he needed to marry her.

She parked next to the chopping block, said hello to Bruno, and unloaded the wood. Not exactly a winter's supply, she thought, but it should serve her present purposes. A lavender haze was settling over the hillside and the air seemed unusually sharp, causing Alex to shiver in her wool suit, sheer stockings and low heeled pumps. Fall was fast approaching. When she'd left this morning she'd noticed the birch leaves had turned yellow. She stood very still and listened to an odd sifting sound that seemed to surround her. It was the sound of leaves dropping to the ground, she realized. Fall had lasted exactly one day.

She lit the kerosene lantern and quickly changed her clothes, reverting back to the braless look that gave Casey a glazed cast to his eyes. She pulled on a pair of tight faded jeans and buttoned herself into a blue shirt. She looked at her reflection in the small oval mirror and wrinkled her nose. Not exactly right. She shrugged out of the shirt and tugged a forest green turtleneck over her head. Better, she decided, tucking it in at the waist. More revealing, less accessible. It would look great with a few flour smudges. Homey and sexy. Manhunting clothes, she thought smugly. After all, this was war. She made biscuit batter, humming happily, and slid the cut dough onto a brand new cookie sheet. She prepared chicken breast filets for frying. Now she had to make it look as if she'd tried to start the woodstove. She purposely used too much paper, not enough kindling, and almost completely closed the damper. Acrid smoke billowed into the cabin, bringing tears to her eyes before she had a chance to douse the fire. "Perfect," she said to Bruno. She strategically placed a flour smudge on her nose and left breast, slipped into her ski parka and set off for Casey's house.

She met him halfway along the wooded trail. "Where are you going?"

Casey scowled at her. "I'm going to your cabin. What the hell are you doing down there, barbecuing your loft?"

Alex blinked at him. "Have you been spying on me?"

"I saw the smoke from my living room window." Through the binoculars he was using to spy on her, he thought. No reason to go into detail. He couldn't see much through the trees anyway. "If the smoke had been coming from your chimney, it would have risen differently."

"Hmmm. Well, I've been making biscuits, but I couldn't figure out the woodstove. I did everything you told me to do, but all I get is smoke. And how do you know if it's the right temperature for biscuits?"

"After you burn a couple hundred you get the hang of it." Casey wiped the flour smudge off Alex's nose and followed her back to the cabin. He paused for a moment to look at the neat pile of split logs. A surprised expression flickered in his eyes and was instantly masked.

The mask remained on his face while he looked around the lamp-lit room. A deep purple African violet plant sat beside the lamp on the round table. Alex had added books to the collection of foodstuffs on the wall shelves, and a multicolored rag rug had been positioned in front of the small chest of drawers. The loft reminded him of a dark cozy nest. She was laying down roots, he thought grimly. This wasn't the house of a woman who intended to leave. This was a home. How long it would be home remained to be seen. It was still warm by Alaskan standards and the living was relatively easy. He squatted in front of the stove and rearranged the wood. "Too much paper, not enough kindling, and your damper was set wrong," he told Alex.

She removed her jacket, knelt down, and leaned against him to get a better look. "Hmmm," she said, pressing her breast into his arm ever so slightly. She felt him go rigid and tried not to smile. "I see what I was doing wrong." She jiggled a flue, which caused her breasts to bounce lightly. He gave her a questioning look, and she immediately stood, biting her lip in embarrassed innocence. "Sorry," she said. "I wasn't thinking." She took a bottle of burgundy from the shelf and poured him a glass of wine. "Payment for fixing my stove. Thank you."

Casey sipped the wine and stared at her. "Don't you ever wear a bra?"

"I'm saving on laundry."

His gaze dropped to her jeans, and she knew he was wondering just how far her frugality went. "Forget it," she said, smiling. "I'm not telling you." She took a black iron skillet from a hook on the wall and set it on the top of the stove. "How about giving me a cooking lesson? I want to fry this chicken."

"Give the fire a couple minutes. You want to do the chicken and the biscuits when it's at its hottest."

Alex poured a glass of wine for herself. "I've decided you were right about us. We aren't suited to each other at all."

Casey slouched in a ladder-back chair. "No?"

She dipped the chicken in an egg, milk, and dijon mustard mixture, and rolled it in spiced breadcrumbs. "No. We have different interests and different life-styles." She took a sip of wine, put a dollop of margarine and an equal amount of oil into the frying pan, and watched it sizzle. "You were smart to realize that." She slid the tray of biscuits into the oven and transferred the chicken to the hot oil. "I think it's important for people to be honest with themselves and not pretend something is what it isn't. What I mean is, it isn't as if we were in love. It was just a little fling, right? Now that it's over we can be good friends. After all, we're neighbors."

"A little fling?"

"Probably we aren't even that well matched in bed."

A frown drew Casey's brows together. "I thought we were pretty well matched."

Alex kept her face averted and carefully turned the pieces of chicken. "I thought so too at the time, but I've been thinking about it, and I've been worrying that it might have just *seemed* good to me because I'm so inexperienced. Probably I should get to know a lot more men before I make a decision like that." She leaned over the table to set a plate for herself and felt her breasts sway under the jersey material. The tips peaked slightly against the abrasion and the dark, watchful eyes of Michael Casey. She let him watch for a moment before turning back to the stove.

"A *lot* more men? How many men is a lot more?"

Alex shrugged. "I don't know. You can't set a number on those things. I suppose you just know when you've had enough." She set a tub of butter and the bottle of wine on the table. "How many women have you had?"

Casey colored under the beginnings of a five o'clock shadow. "Enough."

She put a tossed salad on the table, added a grind of fresh pepper, and looked at Casey, as if a thought had just occurred to her. "Would you like to stay for supper?"

"No. Thank you for asking, but I think I'd better be getting home."

Alex opened the oven door and took out the tray of golden-brown biscuits, flooding the small room with their freshly baked aroma. She dumped them in a breadbasket lined with a white linen napkin and set them steaming on the table.

"That's not fair," Casey said, looking at the tempting biscuits. "You're playing dirty."

"For goodness sakes, Casey, they're only biscuits." She pierced the chicken filets and, deciding they were done, drained them briefly and arranged them on a plate garnished with fresh parsley.

Casey looked as if he might swoon from fried chicken and homemade biscuit fumes. He sat back down in his chair. "Maybe I could stay a little longer."

Alex smiled and set a plate for him. "Good. I have lots of things to ask you, now that we're friends."

"Uh-oh."

"Originally I came here looking for a husband," Alex said, savoring a bite of chicken while she buttered a biscuit. "I'm still on the lookout for the right man, but you know there are all kinds of alternative life-styles for the modern woman now. I don't necessarily have to do it in the traditional order of love, marriage, family. Since the right man hasn't come along, I could reverse the order and have a baby first. I could be artificially inseminated. Then I wouldn't feel so rushed to find a husband. What do you think?"

Casey felt his biscuit lodge in the middle of his throat. Was she serious? She looked serious. "I think . . . I think you're nuts. It's going to be hard enough for you to get through a winter on this mountain without being pregnant." What he meant was it's going to be hard enough for *him* to get through the winter with her on his mountain. He hadn't had a decent night's sleep since she arrived. How would he ever manage to stay sane if she were pregnant?

She waved her fork at him. "You know your problem? You underestimate women."

"Dammit, I don't underestimate women. You underestimate Alaska. Living alone in an unimproved cabin is dangerous, even for a veteran Alaskan. You're a walking time bomb, a disaster waiting to happen."

"Maybe we should change the subject," Alex said. "Do you like the chicken?"

"The chicken's excellent."

"You look grouchy."

"I feel grouchy." He stabbed a piece of raw broccoli. "What are you going to do when the weather drops and your car won't start? Suppose you go into labor in the middle of a snowstorm?"

"I have it all thought out. I'll get inseminated next month, and then I'll have the baby when the weather is nice."

"You're crazy, you know that? Suppose you get sperm from a lunatic?"

"I think they check on those things."

"Yeah, sure. They say to the guy, 'Are you crazy?' And he says no, and then they hand him a little paper cup."

Alex tipped her head back and laughed. "That's

not true. The entire procedure is very scientific and reliable." This was going even better than she'd expected. Casey looked totally frustrated. She decided to push it further. "I thought since I've decided to live in Alaska, I'd try for an Eskimo donor."

"Well, hell, why not go all the way and get musk-ox sperm? That's even more Alaskan."

Alex wrinkled her nose and put a large pot of water on the stove to heat. "If you help me with the dishes, I'll give you dessert."

Casey remembered the last time she gave him dessert and felt a stirring within him. The taste of her still lingered in his mind, hot and achingly sweet. If he closed his eyes, he could feel her flesh under his hands, her belly quivering as he kissed her. . . . Damn. "No more dessert."

Alex flashed him another of her innocent looks of surprise. "Don't you like brownies?" she said, displaying a small white cardboard box of store-bought brownies.

"I guess a brownie would be okay," he answered, reaching for one. He was over the edge. It was that hands-off turtleneck she was wearing. And her perfume. It was the same scent that clung to his pillow, keeping him awake and aroused all night. Not tonight, he vowed. Tonight he was going to sleep like a baby. He was going right home and change his linens. As soon as he had his brownie.

Alex gathered the dishes and plunged them into the sudsy water heating on the stove. She washed and rinsed a plate and handed it to Casey. "This is nice, isn't it? I'm glad we're friends. It makes everything so much easier when all that sexual tension is removed from a relationship."

"What makes you think the sexual tension is removed from our relationship?" he said, drying the plate with a dishtowel.

Alex gave him another dish and threw him her best confused look. "I thought it was obvious. I mean, we tried being lovers, and it didn't work. I assumed we were all ready to move on to bigger and better things."

Casey stopped wiping and stared at her. A crooked smile settled on his mouth and his eyes opened wide in disbelief at her audacity. "Bigger and better things?"

Alex burst out laughing. She hadn't meant it as a double entendre. Michael Casey was a perfect measure on the yardstick of life. "Bigger and better is just an expression." Alex grinned. "It's not meant to be taken literally." She gave him a teasing side-long glance. "Although, now that I think about it—"

Casey grabbed her by the scruff of her neck. "Are you about to insult me?"

Alex yelped and hit him on the head with her wet sponge. Soap suds clung to his hair and dotted his shirt. His eyes darkened and he reached out for her. "You're in trouble now."

"Casey!"

He caught her wrists as she jumped away, walking her backward until she was pressed against the wall. "No one hits Michael Casey in the head with a wet sponge and lives."

Alex felt her heart quicken. "Would another brownie help?"

"An apology would help."

He was so close, she could feel his breath on her mouth. The tips of her breasts grazed Casey's shirt and turned tingling hard. She shifted her weight, bringing her body into even closer contact, causing the tightened nipples to rub against his chest. "Sorry I hit you in the head with the sponge," she murmured.

His eyes were smoky, watching her mouth. "And the insult?"

"I was only thinking of insulting you."

Casey pressed his straining zipper into her. "Maybe I can help you make up your mind. I wouldn't want you to make a wrong decision about me. After all, my reputation is at stake."

Alex struggled to keep her wits. This wasn't part of the plan. She'd intended to remove some of the pressure by feigning disinterest. She'd intended to dangle herself in front of him, not throw herself into his bed. In another minute they'd both be in the loft. It would set a dangerous precedent, and it would ruin her friendly, neighborly facade. If she was going to pull this off, she was going to have to resist. She looked him straight in the eye and kept her voice light. "Can I take this to mean that the sexual tension hasn't entirely disappeared?"

A muscle worked in Casey's jaw. "Not entirely."

Her senses were spinning at his nearness, and she found it hard to give him just a sisterly kiss on the tip of his nose and push him away. "I'm sure it will in time. It's something we'll have to work at if we're going to be friends." She must be mad, she thought, to refuse to surrender to his sensuous mouth and igniting touch.

"Yeah." He wrenched the door open and turned to look at her. "How the hell did you get all that wood chopped?"

Alex put the box of brownies in his hand. "You don't expect me to tell you all my secrets, do you?"

Eight

Arms crossed over her chest, Alex stood motionless, looking out the small square pane of glass in
the back door of her store. A sameness had settled into her life that hinted at the tedium Casey
had warned her about. The first of October had
brought a few snowflakes that settled on rock
hard ground and never melted. In the past two
weeks, snow had intermittently floated down from
a flat leaden sky and accumulated to no more
than an inch or two. It was dry, powdery stuff
that blew away under cars and felt like grit underfoot. She'd discarded her skirts and heels in favor
of long johns, corduroys, hiking boots, and a down
coat. The coat was a source of amusement to
Andy and his cronies. Only thin-blooded newcom-
ers wore down this early in the year. The temperature hadn't even dropped to below zero.

Behind the store an expanse of rutted, snow-covered ground stretched to a birch stand. The trees were ramrod straight, tall and slender, their color muted by a weak sun sitting low in the sky and the fine, almost invisible snow, which had begun to fall. There was a stolid loneliness to the birch trees. They'd shed all their leaves, giving them a stripped-bare look and now had to endure the harsh Alaskan winter. Not even snow clung to them.

Alex felt as if she were a birch tree standing stiff and purposeless. She served no function in the store. She'd memorized catalogues of fishing equipment and shotgun shells, but business was never brisk enough to occupy two people at once, and the men obviously preferred to talk to Andy. Only one sale from the new stock of cross-country skis had been made. And that was to Bubba Johanssen whose small natural foods store was on the same highway as Alex's store. Like good neighbors, they patronized each other's businesses.

She felt lonely having no friends for companionship. That traitor, Bruno, had taken to living with Casey. In the beginning she'd trudged up the hill to retrieve the dog, but as the weeks passed she'd left him more and more in Casey's care. It had simply become too painful to intrude on Casey's privacy. He'd rebuked all overtures of friendship, declining casual dinner invitations, finding excuses not to invite her in when she visited his house to inquire about Bruno or to ask advice.

Well, hell, she thought, her mouth narrow with

grim determination, she'd go right on standing there like the damn birch trees. Casey and Bruno could go take a hike for all she cared. She wasn't giving up. She'd still be here when spring came, and who knew, maybe she'd flower.

She suddenly realized darkness had settled around her. The birch trees were no longer visible behind the thick veil of snow that fell outside.

Andy flicked the lights on in the store. "Lord, are you still here? I thought you left hours ago. Don't you know better than to wait for the snow to build up?"

Alex looked at him blank faced. No, she didn't know better than to wait for the snow to build up. She didn't know much of anything. "It's been snowing for weeks. I didn't see any difference—"

"There's a big difference. This here's a storm. Look at the the size of them flakes."

"You think traveling will be bad?"

"Traveling won't be bad in an Alaskan car, but it ain't gonna be so hot in your worthless little New Jersey car. You got friends in town here? Someone you can stay with?"

"No," she answered dully, "I don't have any friends." She took her down coat from a peg on the wall. "I'm sure if I leave now I'll be fine."

Andy shook his head. "I don't think that's a good idea."

But Alex went out anyway, and two hours later she came to a stop on the two-lane road and released her white-knuckled grip on the steering wheel. She rotated her head to relax neck muscles and peered into the swirling snow that swept over the hood of the little car. Her driveway was just ahead, nothing more than a gash in the black woods, and she knew it was ridiculous to think she could navigate the grade. It would be fool-hardy to turn back; the road was quickly disap-pearing. The driveway at least looked traveled. Casey had obviously been through with his four-wheel drive. She would have to get as far as possi-ble in her car and walk the rest of the way to her cabin. She wasn't surprised when she slid on the first curve and settled into a drift.

Casey stood in his darkened living room and looked out at a familiar world. He'd lived just about his whole life in Alaska and knew by arctic standards this wasn't much of a storm. The Fair-banks area was located between two mountain ranges and didn't get the heavy, drifting snows found on the coast. The weather was holding at five degrees below zero, not low enough to stop school buses from running or damage his insu-lated plumbing. Then why was his stomach tied in knots, as it had been for weeks? Because Alex was out there in the storm somewhere. He'd checked on her cabin every half hour since the storm had begun. He wanted to believe she'd stayed at the store, but instinct told him otherwise. Bruno sensed it too, prowling by the plate-glass window, his ears pricked. Casey scratched the dog's head. "You're worried too, aren't you, fella?"

Casey had encouraged Bruno to stay with him. He'd wanted Alex to be lonely, so lonely she'd leave.

Every day she stayed was an agony for him. He couldn't live with her, and he couldn't live without her. It took every ounce of willpower he possessed to avoid her. Knowing she was less than a quarter mile through the birches was torture. When she left each morning, he secretly added logs to her dwindling woodpile and checked to make sure she had enough kerosene. Every evening he waited at the tree line until he was sure she was safe and snug for the night. He dreamed of having her in his bed, his mouth on hers, his hands caressing her, and . . . When it was all he could do to keep from rushing to her side, he retreated to his house where he cursed himself for being a fool and getting involved. Now he cursed himself for stealing Bruno from her. At least Bruno would have been another warm body. A dog could be a valuable ally in a snowstorm.

Casey kept vigil in the dark to better see outdoors. He watched for a glimmer of light on the road, on the driveway, in her cabin. It was seven o'clock. If there was no sign of her by seven-thirty, he'd make another sweep of the driveway and head for College.

It had been a long arduous uphill walk. Alex knew she had accomplished it only because Casey had packed the snow with his truck tires. Her white woolen hat was encrusted with snow, which also clung to her frozen pant legs. She'd wrapped the matching scarf around the lower part of her face, but her thick lashes held a layer of hoary frost, and her high cheekbones were chalky white with frostbite. If she hadn't been so bone-tired, she would have realized the folly of wading through her unplowed drive and stayed on the main road to Casey's house. But the cold was making her mentally and physically slow. She put her head down and doggedly plodded on through snow that had accumulated knee-high.

She drifted onto the shoulder of her driveway, stumbled, and fell face first, cursing her stupidity because she'd lost her hat and didn't have the energy to look for it. She pulled herself up and forced herself to continue walking, channeling her reserves to become more alert. She fell once more, but her cabin was within sight. You're almost there, she told herself, just a few feet from hot chocolate, a cozy fire in the big woodstove, woolen socks, and warm long johns. She pounded on her thighs to keep blood circulating in her hands and legs, and staggered the distance to her door.

Her cabin was only a few degrees warmer inside than it was outside, but there wasn't any snow and there wasn't any wind. She pulled her snow-encrusted mittens off with her teeth and tried to start the kerosene heater, but her fingers were frozen and clumsy in the stygian darkness. A frustrated, distraught sob caught in her throat and was immediately replaced with an angry expletive. She was angry because Casey had been right. She was a disaster waiting to happen. She placed her stiff hands under her armpits to thaw. Gritting her teeth, she jumped up and down, swearing that Casey wasn't going to have the satisfaction of finding her dead.

She tried the heater again and gave a cry of relief when her fingers did all the right things and the machine began to put out heat into the room. She lit the lantern on her table and felt much better now that she had light. Alexandra Scott, hardy pioneer of the Alaskan frontier, had saved herself from almost certain death, she thought. She mustered up a little false bravado and told herself there was nothing to this survival business. She began to undress, but decided it would be prudent to visit her outhouse before snuggling into her jammies.

Casey closed his eyes and leaned his forehead against the triple-paned window when he saw the weak glimmer of a light winking through the tops of the birch trees. He drew in a shaky breath and switched on his own lights, including the big floodlights on the outside deck and garage. Emotions were pounding through him as he shrugged into his parka. Anger, relief, remnants of anxiety. He didn't know whether he wanted to sweep Alex into his arms and let his love pour into her, or grab her by her shoulders and shake her until her teeth rattled.

He'd reached the tree line when he heard the eerie hiss of burning wood and saw the yellow flames shooting high into the air. He broke into a run, the snow dragging at his boots and pant legs, blind fear clogging his throat. He stopped short when he recognized the slim figure silhouetted by the blaze. Her hair was in total disarray, sticking out every which way, snow rapidly collecting on singed tips. She wore no coat, but she wasn't shivering. The heat of the fire was enough to warm her, as she placidly stared into the inferno with trancelike contemplation.

Casey watched her for a moment before speaking. "Should we break out the marshmallows?"

"I haven't got any."

He saw that her hair was considerably shorter and took a deep breath to control the tremble he was afraid would surface in his voice. "What happened to your hair?"

"I suppose it caught fire," Alex answered matter-of-factly. "I burned down my outhouse."

"I've noticed. How did you manage this?"

"I had a little candle on the shelf, but my hands were cold when I tried to light it, and before I knew it the toilet paper was burning, and then my jacket caught fire. I guess my hair must have been on fire too. I ran outside and took my jacket off and rolled in the snow." She turned glazed eyes to him. "I'm fine now, except I didn't get to use the outhouse. Do you suppose I could borrow your bathroom?"

Casey had his jaw clenched so tightly the bones in his face ached. He removed his jacket and helped her into it. He zipped it all the way up to her neck and pulled the hood over her smoking hair. Staring at her eyes, he felt a hungry yearning pulse deep within him, and he had to fight the strong urge to pull her to him and cover her face with kisses. Instead he grabbed her by the upper arm and briskly tugged her up the hill to his house. He was afraid to talk to her and say something he'd regret, like beg her to marry him, afraid he'd burst into tears because she'd almost been killed. He led her inside and set her on the couch where he pulled off her boots. Her feet were white and frozen, just as he'd expected. He added a log to the fire and brought her a thick blanket. "I'm going back down the hill to make sure the fire's out," he said. "Get out of those clothes and wrap yourself in the blanket. Your feet are going to hurt when they thaw. Keep them warm and rub them very gently. Will you be all right?"

Alex gave him a thumbs-up. She figured she'd be all right as long as she didn't look in a mirror. She wiggled her toes and gingerly walked to the bathroom, amazed at her state of mind. She'd almost frozen to death. She'd almost gone up in a blaze of glory in her outhouse. Why wasn't she depressed? Why wasn't she crying and shaking? She studied her sooty reflection and grinned because she looked ridiculous and because she was pleased at her resilience. And because it was so obvious how much Casey cared for her, no matter how hard he tried to hide it. Her skin still tingled where he had touched it; her mind savored the memory of how longingly he had looked at her.

By the time Casey had reached the clearing, the fire had burned itself out. He kicked snow on the embers until he was satisfied it posed no threat to the surrounding woods or nearby cabin. He quickly chose some clothes for Alex and extinguished the heater and lantern. Maybe she'd finally realize she didn't belong here and leave. If she didn't, he was going to have to find a way to get her off the mountain.

Alex was fresh from a shower when Casey returned. "Thank you," she replied breezily, accepting the bundle of clothing, clutching a towel to her chest.

He'd expected to come back and find her despondent. Her cheerfulness grated on him. "What the hell are you so happy about? You damn near killed yourself."

She dropped the towel and stepped into a pair of lavender lace panties. "Damn near doesn't count."

Casey felt his stomach tighten at the sight of her. Heat surged through his groin, white hot and fiercely demanding, and a wave of disgust washed over him at his inability to control his reaction to her. He pressed his lips together and turned on his heel, long angry strides carrying him to the front door.

Alex followed him, buttoning an oversized blue cotton shirt. "Where are you going?"

"I'm spending the night in your cabin. And you're to stay here. If you so much as take a step outdoors on those freshly thawed feet, I swear I'll . . ."

Alex looked at him expectantly.

He shook his head. Didn't anything intimidate

this woman? He took his parka and slammed the door behind him.

Alex stared at the kegs of rusty nails and bolts and decided they were going to go. She'd never seen anyone so much as look at them, much less buy any, and she could use the floor space for the new line of cross-country ski equipment. She was feeling guardedly optimistic about the store. This week she'd actually been able to contribute something intelligent to a discussion about hunting bears. She didn't have any experience, but she'd studied the catalogues and knew all the latest hype and statistics on large gauge guns. The men were beginning to include her in their conversations, and yesterday a woman had come in to buy a birthday present for her husband. Alex considered it a milestone.

Unfortunately, the positive feelings she held about the store were partially dampened by the fact that her personal life was a shambles. Casey was doggedly ignoring her again; he hadn't said more than five words to her since that night almost a week ago when she'd burned down her outhouse. She decided she was going to have to be patient and wear him down with her persistence. She'd just hang in there, and in twenty-five or thirty years he'd come around. Her eyes flew open when a vaguely familiar figure entered the store.

"Holy cow, will ya look at this," Harry Kowalski

said, his wheezy voice laced with disgust. "Lord, girl, what have you done to the place? It used to be so homey." He looked at Alex more closely. "And you done something odd to your hair. Looks like one of them spikey styles you see on those New Jersey weirdos. Especially the part where it gets orange at the frizzy tips." The old man squinted at the freshly painted walls and new light fixtures and shook his head. "I suppose you got Andy all gussied up wearing a suit."

"She ain't got Andy wearing nothin'," Andy said from the doorway of the back room. "What are you doing here, you old coot?"

"Hell, I couldn't stand New Jersey. Too many people. Too many cars. I couldn't figure out how to work half the gadgets in the kitchen. Everything was electric. Nothing smelled like wood smoke. And when you set on the can and open the door you don't see nothing but carpet." He turned to Alex. "You swindled me. You took advantage of an old man."

She felt her mouth drop open. "*I* took advantage of you? You neglected to mention the fact that your driveway had trees growing in it. And you conveniently forgot to tell me that your cabin lacked water, plumbing, heat, and electricity."

"Well, of course it don't have none of those things. That's why you call it a cabin in the woods. Now if I told you I had a fancy condo, it would have been something else."

Alex crossed her arms over her chest and narrowed her eyes.

"Anyway, the deal's off," Harry said. "I want my house back. I don't like New Jersey."

"Too bad," Alex told him. "I don't like New Jersey either."

"But you aren't an old man. It'll be easy for you to find someplace else to live. That there cabin's my home, and I'm homesick. I'll give you the deed back to your condo if you'll give me my cabin back."

"No way. Those monthly payments were killing me."

Harry hung his head and wiped his nose with a big cloth handkerchief. "I been on that mountain for more years than I can remember. But I guess you're right. I made the mistake, and now I got to live with it. It's just that sometimes you don't know how much you love something until you don't have it. I never had a wife or family. All I had was that cabin."

Alex held her hand up. "Stop. Enough." She bowed her head and sighed. "I know when I'm licked. Man, I'm such a sucker for a sob story. You can live in the cabin, but I don't want the condo."

"Hope you haven't ruined the cabin too," Harry said.

"Afraid so. I've gotten rid of all the mice and mold. You'll just have to tough it out for a while." It wasn't really such a loss, Alex thought. Casey had been right; it was impractical for her to live on the mountain in the winter. Her little car couldn't navigate the steep, winding driveway in the snow. If she got a sturdier one, she would still be faced with the problem of the cold. Twice this week she'd needed a jump start from Casey. She now knew the value of the wire and plug that dangled from the hood of Alaskan cars. The wire was attached to an engine heater. When the weather turned cold, cars had to be plugged into outdoor receptacles before they could be driven. Since she had no electricity she was left with the homesteaders' solution to the problem . . . remove the battery from the car and bring it into the cabin each night. Not something she looked forward to doing.

Harry took an oatmeal cookie from the cookie jar. "How soon do you suppose I could move in? I ain't got no place to stay, you know."

"You can stay with Andy."

"No way," Andy said. "Not enough room for two people. I can hardly turn around in there myself."

It was true, Alex thought, the room was small. A smile spread across her mouth. She had the solution to the problem. "Andy, you can move into the cabin with Harry, and I'll live here. It would be easy to build a bunk under the loft bed for you."

Andy crossed his arms over his chest. "I'm used to living alone. I got all my things here."

The authoritative executive surfaced under the punk haircut. "We'll move your things. Take it or leave it," Alex told him, her tone leaving no doubt in anyone's mind that she was serious.

Several hours later, Alex stuffed the last of her

clothes and other possessions into packing boxes, which she tied to her car as best she could. She carefully maneuvered up the treacherous drive to Casey's house to leave him a note of explanation and collect Bruno.

Casey was out, but the door was unlocked as usual. Alex stepped out of her snowy boots and prowled the kitchen in search of paper and pencil, noting that Casey's housekeeping habits had taken a turn for the worse. Fast-food boxes were everywhere. A Tupperware container had melted on the toaster. A saucepan, its bottom black and scorched, had stuck onto one of the electrical coils on the stove top. Half-filled coffee cups sat on end tables, window sills, bookshelves, and countertops. A stack of mail was spread across the butcher-block work island.

Alex rifled through the opened envelopes and loose correspondence, hoping to find something she could write on. A bill from a travel agency caught her eye. It was for airfare from New Jersey to Fairbanks. It required little insight to add up the facts. Casey had bought Harry's ticket. The knowledge rushed through her cold and hard. She couldn't move. She could barely breathe. The silence in the house felt crushing. It had never occurred to her that Casey would go this far to get rid of her.

She stood there for a long while, absorbing the information, trying to come to terms with the hurt it caused. Casey had good reason to want her off the mountain, she decided. She was a menace. She'd torched her outhouse. That was the least of it. In Casey's eyes she represented a high-risk marriage. If she were in his shoes, she might be acting the same way. It must be terrible to have your child taken away from you.

She reviewed her life and realized she'd never experienced a loss of that magnitude. She was born and raised in a small town in New Jersey. Her parents still lived there. Her life had held no traumatic illnesses, no tragic deaths, few crushing disappointments. The break-up of her engagement had been humiliating but surprisingly painless. The demise of her relationship with Casey wouldn't be nearly so bland. The thought of living without him left her hollow inside. The thought of living with him made her furious. He'd dragged an old man five thousand miles to get her out of her cabin.

She felt a smile poking around inside of her. Casey should pay for this. With his life. With matrimony. No way was she giving up now. She'd make him a terrific wife—whether he wanted one or not. The smile surfaced on her lips and glinted fiendishly in her eyes as she swung the patio door open and began bringing her boxes into Casey's house.

Casey pulled into his driveway and saw Alex's car loaded with the packing boxes. It had worked. She was leaving. No, wait a minute, she wasn't leaving, she was moving in! He bolted from his truck and caught Alex unpacking a box of lingerie. "What are you doing?"

Alex put on her most innocent face. "You'll never guess what happened. Harry came back today."

"No."

"Yes. The poor thing was homesick. He was so pitiful, Casey. He really doesn't want much from life. All he wants is to be able to live out his old age in that sad little cabin."

"And?"

"Well, of course I had to give it back to him. How could I possibly refuse?"

"And?"

"At first I was going to make Andy move in with Harry, so I could live in Andy's room behind the store." She shook out a filmy black lace camisole and refolded it. "But that wouldn't be fair to Andy. He feels the same way about that grungy room as Harry feels about the cabin. So I decided I would look for a small apartment in town."

Casey felt panic as he watched the pile of sexy garments grow. "Are you going to put those in my bedroom?"

"Harry was determined to move right into his cabin, which leaves me with no roof over my head for a while. It takes time to find the perfect apartment. I mean, I can't just move into the first thing that comes along."

"About your undies . . ."

"I noticed you have some room left over in your sock drawer."

"You're putting that black lacy thing in my sock drawer?" His voice had grown unusually shrill.

"Just until I find the perfect apartment. You

see, I had this terrific idea while I was moving out of my cabin. I thought since you and Harry were such good friends, and since this happened so suddenly—" And since you probably feel guilty about doing this, she silently added "—I thought you wouldn't mind if I bunked here for a while."

Casey was dumbfounded. He hadn't considered the possibility of this happening. When he'd persuaded Harry to con Alex out of the cabin, he'd been sure it would get her off the mountain. Instead it had gotten her into his house! "Hell."

"Pardon?" Alex asked, inwardly quaking with laughter.

"I don't think this is such a good idea."

Alex retrieved another carton from her car. "It's only temporary. I have it all figured out. I'll take care of your house, cooking and cleaning, in exchange for room and board." She dumped the contents of the box on the living room floor and began sorting out blue and orange tent struts.

"Going camping?"

"Yup. This is terrific idea number two. I'll set my tent up in the corner behind the fireplace, and it will make a cozy bedroom for me. You won't even know I'm here. This is going to work out just fine. Don't worry about a thing. Oh, and by the way, I have a date tonight, so don't be concerned if I come home kind of late."

"You have a *date* tonight?"

Alex's stomach fluttered at the quietly incredulous tone of the question. "Not exactly a date. I promised Bubba Johanssen I'd show him how to wax his new cross-country skis."

"That should take about ten minutes."

Alex agreed. "But then he's going to take me out with his sled team. He's going to show me how to be a musher!"

Casey tried to remember what sort of butt Bubba Johanssen had been blessed with, but the image eluded him. It wasn't the sort of thing he ordinarily noticed.

Nine

Bubba was tall and broad and blond. His features were common, not good-looking, not bad-looking, simply ordinary. In fact, everything about him was pleasantly ordinary. He was several years younger than Alex, and if she had to describe her relationship with Bubba, she would say it was comfortably platonic.

He guided his jeep up the twisting drive to Casey's house with casual expertise, all the while explaining the intricacies of raising a dog team. "You have to give the dogs more oil and protein in the winter," he said. "I like to mix a lot of fish and some eggs into my dog food. I dip net salmon in the summer, then I slice off a few steaks for myself and use the rest for the dogs."

Drowsy, Alex listened to him. The sled ride had been exhilarating with the cold air biting at her face and the dogs yipping in front of her. The snow had shone eerily white as a full moon rose in the indigo sky, and Alex skimmed along the packed powder of Bubba's route, riding the runners, shouting "hike" like a seasoned musher. She'd been dumped twice when she'd attempted to apply the brake, and the snow she'd acquired on the ruff of her hood and woolen mittens was melting in the heat of the car. She nodded politely, only partially folllowing Bubba's conversation, caught in the lethargy that came after playing hard in the snow.

Casey didn't turn from the television when she came in, but he listened to her footsteps. She went to the bathroom, to his bedroom—what the devil was she doing in his bedroom? Then she sauntered into the kitchen to pour a glass of juice. From the corner of his eyes he could see that she'd changed from heavy sweater and ski pants to a pastel rugby shirt and jeans.

"Casey," she called, "you want anything from the kitchen?"

"No."

She flopped onto the other end of the couch and looked at the TV with unseeing eyes.

Casey drummed his fingers on the arm of the couch. In his opinion Alexandra Scott looked altogether too pleased, like the cat that swallowed the canary. She was supposed to have gone out to wax skis, for crying out loud. Waxing skis had never been such a rewarding, exhausting experience for *him*. Finally he turned and stared at her. "Why are you smiling like that?"

Alex hadn't been aware of the smile, but she was aware of feeling very happy. She was living with Casey, and she'd discovered an Alaskan activity that she genuinely liked—mushing. The fire crackled and hissed in the fireplace, the TV droned on, and the refrigerator hummed. Everything around her felt very much like home. "Am I smiling? Hmmm." She yawned and stretched. "I'm pooped. I'm going to bed." She kissed him on the tip of his nose, patted him on the top of the head, and walked to her tent.

It's a nightmare, Casey thought. This isn't really happening. I'm going to be very calm, and I'm going to go to bed. Maybe I'll have a drink first. Maybe I'll have lots of drinks. Maybe I'll take the bottle into the bedroom with me. He slouched a little lower, wondering if she'd been kissed, wondering if she was still on her insane husband hunt . . . or worse, trying to get pregnant.

Casey was awake, but he couldn't open his eyes. Something was stomping around inside his head, and his eyes felt like fried eggs. He knew if he opened them in bright daylight, they'd explode. He had a vague memory of drinking a lot of Scotch and of not being able to remove his jeans. He felt around and verified the fact. Yup, he still had them on. The thought occurred to him that he probably could have taken them off last night if he had removed his hiking boots first. His heart skipped a beat at the sound of the shower running. He lived alone. Who was in the shower? He opened one eye in time to see a woman clad in a small towel rifling through his sock drawer. Oh god, it was Alex. How could he have forgotten?

"Morning," she said cheerfully.

"Mmmf."

She twirled a scrap of red lace around her finger and waltzed out of the room. "Breakfast in fifteen minutes."

Was she kidding? He'd die if he smelled breakfast. He was still contemplating dying when Alex brought him a cup of coffee.

"Anybody home?" Alex said, tapping Casey on the forehead with her index finger.

Casey gave her a black look and slowly moved to a sitting position. He took a sip of coffee and let it roll around in his mouth.

"Had a nightcap, huh?"

"It's you," Casey growled. "You're driving me to drink."

"Oh, yeah, well, next time I'll drive you some place else. You look like hell."

Casey made an unintelligible sound deep in his throat.

"I'd like to stay and exchange grunts with you, but I have to get to work. There's a full pot of coffee in the kitchen and some stick-to-your-ribs oatmeal."

Casey clapped his hand over his mouth, and Alex saw beads of sweat pop out on his forehead.

"Not ready for oatmeal, huh? I'll cover it, and you can nuke it later when your stomach is up to it."

When Casey got home at six o'clock, Alex was busy in the kitchen. She removed a casserole from the oven and set it steaming and fragrant on the dining room table. She handed Casey a large bowl of salad and slid a loaf of hot French bread onto a breadboard. "Hungry?" she asked.

Casey shrugged. He was starving! He hadn't had anything to eat all day and the casserole was making him drool, but he had to be cool. He didn't want her to feel too appreciated. He didn't want her to get the wrong idea and think he was enjoying this cohabitation stuff. Actually he was enjoying it just a little, he admitted, but he also hated it. It was unnatural to have a woman sleeping in a tent in your living room. Especially when you wanted her to be sleeping in your bed. And every time he reached into his drawer for a pair of socks, he was confronted with her panties.

"Are you all right?" Alex set a goblet of ice tea in front of Casey. "You look a little strange."

"It's the panties—" His face colored. "I mean, it's the casserole. I didn't expect you to go to all this trouble."

Alex sat opposite him and spread her napkin on her lap. "We made a deal. Room and board in exchange for my housewifely services."

Casey's fork stopped midway to his mouth.

"No need to get alarmed. It's simply an expression." She spooned some casserole onto her plate. "And of course, it's not to be confused with conjugal privileges. I know you'll be relieved at that. We're just two good friends sharing a house for a while, aren't we? Personally, I like it. It's comfy, you know? Oh, and by the way, I'm going to help Bubba oil his harnesses tonight. I shouldn't be too late."

Casey's grip tightened on his fork. He stuffed a chunk of meat into his mouth and chewed vigorously.

Five hours later, Casey heard Alex stomping the snow off her boots on the deck and quickly buried his nose in the mystery he was reading. He'd been on page fifty-seven for two hours and didn't have a clue what it said. Last night it had been waxing skis until ten, and this night it had been oiling harnesses until eleven. Not that it was any of his business. If she was interested in Bubba Johanssen, then good for her. Let Johanssen be left high and dry when she took off. Let Johanssen mail his kid's Christmas presents to New Jersey. I should be happy she's found someone else, Casey told himself. But he wasn't happy; he was damned furious.

She entered and he saw she was smiling again. "Had a good time?" he asked tersely.

Alex hung her jacket on the wall and stepped out of her boots. "The best! I got to feed the dogs tonight. I'm going back tomorrow, and Bubba's going to let me drive his four-dog racing team."

She tweaked Casey's nose, said good night, and crawled into her tent.

It was enough to drive him nuts.

The moon was high in the sky when Bubba parked his truck in Casey's driveway and walked Alex to the front door. "What you really want to look for in a sled dog is good feet," he said. "The pads have to be tough."

Casey opened the door even before they reached it and pulled Alex inside. "It's twelve-fifteen," he said. "Did you know that?"

Alex's cheeks were flushed, her eyes still glowing from the evening's sport. "Casey, I drove the racing team tonight, and I didn't tip over once. Bubba said I was a natural."

"I'll just bet he did," Casey growled, glowering at Bubba.

Bubba stuffed his hands into his pockets and grinned. "He sure is cranky," he said to Alex. "You have a curfew or something?"

"He's tired," Alex said. "It's past his bedtime."

"Well, hell, Casey, you don't have to stay up on our account." Bubba slung his arm around Alex's shoulders. "Alex is going to make me some cocoa, and I'm going to tell her all about my breeding potential."

"First Eskimos, then musk-ox, now this half-baked musher . . . that does it," Casey said through clenched teeth. "You can take your breeding potential and stick it up your—" Smack! Casey punched Bubba in the nose.

Bubba shook his head to clear it, uttered an expletive and grabbed Casey by the neck. In an instant they were rolling on the carpet and throwing punches.

Alex couldn't believe her eyes. It was the first real fist fight she'd ever seen. "Stop it!" she shouted. "Stop it this instant!" She attempted to grab Bubba and pull him away but was batted off like a fly and sent sprawling on the floor. Blood spurted from Bubba's nose; some trickled from a cut over Casey's eye. It would have been horrible and frightening if it hadn't been so ridiculous and childish. "It took me two hours to get this living room in order," she told the brawling men, "and now you're getting blood all over my clean carpet." Bubba gave Casey a knee to the groin, and Casey poked his finger in Bubba's eye. "That's it," Alex said, stomping off to the bedroom. She drew a line across her throat. "I've had it up to here with this." She returned with Casey's loaded forty-four magnum. She pointed the gun at the ceiling and squeezed the trigger. A loud bang resounded throughout the house. The kick from the gun sent Alex to her knees, and a large chunk of plaster dropped onto Casey's head. The men stopped fighting and stared at Alex.

"Out," she said to Bubba. "Out, out, out!" She took a plastic bag from a kitchen drawer, filled it with snow from the deck, and handed it to him. "I hope your nose isn't broken, but if it is, Casey will be happy to pay all your medical expenses."

Casey stood up and dusted plaster out of his hair. "Just don't expect me to pay maternity."

Bubba took the snow from Alex and hurried to the door. "He's crazy," he said. "You're living with a crazy person."

"He's just confused," Alex told Bubba. "He's been under a lot of strain lately."

She found Casey in the bathroom, staring at his puffy eye. "That was the most disgusting display of childish behavior I've ever seen," Alex said to Casey's reflection. "What did you think you were doing?"

"I don't know," Casey said, his voice churlish. "I'm just confused and I've been under a lot of strain lately."

"You need more sleep."

"Hah! Who's fault is that? How am I supposed to get my sleep when you're off running around the countryside with Bubba discussing breeding techniques?"

"If I didn't know better I'd think you were jealous."

"That's ridiculous."

"Anyway, we were talking about breeding techniques in dogs," Alex said.

"I knew that."

"It's important to match up the right dogs so you get good feet and stuff." Alex soaked a washcloth and dabbed at the eye. "You're lucky this doesn't need stitches."

"Do you realize since the first moment I saw you I've been a bloody mess? I've been knocked unconscious, had my nose bashed, my eye gashed. How long are you going to be living here? Maybe I should take out more medical insurance."

Alex taped a Band-Aid across the cut. Better get family coverage, she thought with a tight smile, I'm here to stay. She turned on her heel and exited the bathroom. "I'm tired," she announced. "I'm going to bed. Good night." She shut off every light in the kitchen and living room, crawled into her tent, and turned on a lamp.

Casey stood in the hall, rooted to the spot, watching Alex's silhouette. She pulled off her sweater and slowly removed her bra. Then she stretched and arched her back like a satisfied cat, the action displaying the fullness of her breasts and a slim rib cage. She removed socks and writhed out of jeans and long johns. Casey held his breath while panties were discarded and she moved to her hands and knees to smooth out a wrinkle in the sleeping bag.

Casey felt the blood hot in his veins, pounding through his heart, burning in his groin. He wondered if the striptease had been purposely done for him, the thought only increasing his anger and frustration. He moved toward the tent and stopped, swearing softly. He was out of control, and he was not in a gentle mood. The light snapped off in the tent, and Alex rustled in the sleeping bag. The knowledge of her naked body sliding into the silky bag pushed him over the edge. He uttered a sigh of resignation and in one swift movement unzipped the tent's front flap and pulled her sleeping bag out of the tent. "Always sleep in the nude?" he asked.

Her eyes flew open, and she was startled when she suddenly found herself face to face with Casey. She felt her heart beating in her throat, the air trapped in her lungs. She licked dry lips and tried to speak, but no words came out. She'd wanted to tease him. She knew he'd been watching. But she hadn't expected this!

His hand tore at the bag's zipper, leaving Alex fully exposed. Moonlight poured through the large southward windows, spilling over her parted thighs. Her breasts lifted up to him with each breath, the dark tips hardening as he watched. In her mind, they were married and had been from the very beginning. She smiled—because she was pleased with her life, pleased with her newfound boldness and confidence, and pleased with her ability to love.

It was the smile that was Casey's undoing. It was a Mona Lisa smile—enigmatic, satisfied, warm, womanly. He was suffused with a myriad of fiercely tender emotions that erased all anger and fueled his passion. He wrapped her in his arms and carried her to his bed where their bodies entwined. Bringing each other again and again to ecstacy, they discovered the breathtaking rhythm that left them spent with throbbing passion.

• • •

Casey was quiet at the breakfast table, wrestling with private thoughts. Alex sipped coffee across from him, also lost in contemplation, her silence feeding his bewilderment. The magic of the evening had disappeared with the moonlight, Casey regretfully concluded, and now they were left with reality in bright sunlight. What was the reality? That all his elaborate plans to remove her from his life had gone awry, and he was back at square one. That they had made beautiful love but hadn't solved a single problem. He pushed his breakfast aside, slopping coffee onto the saucer. "This isn't going to work," he said. "You're going to have to leave. Today."

Alex looked up in surprise. "I have nowhere to go."

"Maybe you should go home . . . to New Jersey." He pushed away from the table and took a set of keys from the kitchen counter. I'm going in to the office. I'd appreciate it if you would clear out before I get back."

Alex looked at him calmly. "You'll regret my leaving. You'll miss me."

Casey put on his parka. "I know that. I'll just have to learn to live with it."

At four o'clock Casey came home to a familiar scene. Alex's little car was in his driveway, loaded with packing boxes. He'd finally succeeded. She was leaving. There was no elation in the victory, only bitter disappointment as he realized that deep down inside he'd wanted her to fight to stay. With a small shock he acknowledged that he'd been setting up tests for her, forcing her to prove herself to him. He'd made her face one too many tests, he thought sadly, kicking the snow from his boots before entering the house. He stood with his hands in his pockets, silently watching her.

The silence grated on her. She'd been fuming all day about his insistence that she leave. Just once she'd like to spend the night with this man and wake up to a doting lover. "Nothing to say?"

He had everything to say, but it was stuck inside him, and he was scared to death to let it out.

"Well, I have something to say. I'm not as dumb as you think. I know you brought Harry up here to get me off your damn mountain."

He looked surprised for a moment, then his face hardened. "It was for your own good."

"Well, thank you, but don't do me any favors. I can take care of myself."

"Get serious. You burned down your outhouse."

"Big deal. I make one little mistake, and you take it upon yourself to run me off your mountain."

"One little mistake?" Casey shouted. "Do you know what I found this morning? A gray hair. It's from worrying about you. And I'm probably getting an ulcer. My stomach is a mess."

"Your stomach is a mess from eating fast food. Why don't you stop worrying about me and start worrying about yourself. If you don't watch your step, you're going to end up like Andy and Harry, living here alone, rattling around in a house filled with pizza cartons, Styrofoam burger boxes and crushed beer cans."

Alex snapped a leash onto Bruno's collar and pushed past Casey, not remembering she was in her stockinged feet until she was standing ankle-deep in snow on the deck. She retrieved her boots, stuffed her wet feet into them and hauled Bruno into the little car. She'd like nothing better than to stay and argue with Casey. She was in the mood for a good shouting match, but she had no time, so she threw him one last haughty look and took off down the hill, recklessly fishtailing on the slippery road.

She was going to kill herself, Casey decided. She drove like a maniac. She would undoubtedly get herself into an accident and then he'd have to rescue her, just like always. A smile quirked the corners of his mouth because he knew he'd never really rescued her. She wasn't exactly the frail, helpless type, he thought, getting into his car and carefully following her down the driveway. He found her a quarter mile from the road, tapping her foot on the packed snow, glaring at her car buried nose first in a drift. "Need some help?" Casey asked.

"No."

Casey let the Bronco inch away.

"Wait!" Alex shouted. "I need help. I need a ride into town."

Casey waded through the snow and retrieved

the boxes, packing them into the back of his car. Bruno and Alex slid onto the seat next to Casey.

"Where are we going?" Casey asked.

"To the store . . . and then to the airport."

It was a silent drive to College. It was the second time in five years that Casey had lost someone he desperately loved. First his son, and now Alex. It was worse this time because he knew what was ahead. He already knew about the quiet wanting and the emptiness. He already knew he'd never forget her. The pain wouldn't stab at him so sharply after a while; it would fade to a dull ache, but it would never completely disappear.

Alex directed Casey to unload the boxes at the store. She handed Bruno's leash over to Andy and glanced at her watch.

Casey caught the gesture. "What time does your plane leave?"

"Seven."

His answer was terse. "We can make it."

Alex closed her eyes and relaxed while he drove. She went over a mental checklist in her mind. Her small suitcase was in the back, plane reservations were in her shoulder bag, Andy was caring for Bruno. She was jolted against her seat belt when Casey pulled the car to the shoulder and screeched to a stop.

"Dammit, I never figured you for a quitter," he said. His voice was harsh and his eyes were icy and narrowed. "How could you work so hard to make something liveable and then give it up just like that?" He snapped his fingers.

"Are you talking about my cabin?"

"Your cabin, your store, your whole life. Why are you going back to New Jersey? Why the hell are you going back to the Oreo cookies and one-percent milk? I thought you hated all that?"

Alex opened her mouth to speak, but he interrupted. "Listen, so you trashed your outhouse. It could have happened to anyone."

"I thought you wanted me to leave."

Casey sighed wearily. "I don't know what I wanted. I was scared."

"What about now? Do you know what you want now?"

"I want you. Forever and ever. You think that plane to New Jersey has room for one more passenger? I know this sounds dumb, but I love you more than Alaska. If you want to live someplace else, I'm ready to move."

"I don't want to live any place else. I love Alaska. And I'm not going to New Jersey."

A muscle quivered at his jaw. "Where are you going?"

"I have an appointment in San Francisco. I'm going to get—"

"Oh, man," he said, "you're not going to get pregnant, are you? Don't tell me you still want an Eskimo baby."

Alex rolled her eyes. "No, I'm not going to get pregnant. I'm going to get my hair done."

Casey leaned back and stared at her. "Let me get this straight. You're going to San Francisco for a haircut?"

"It's important to get a good cut. You don't think I'd let just anyone do my hair." She gave him a smug, sideways glance. "It's a treat. I sold a seven hundred dollar rifle to Gordon Newfarmer this week in exchange for my oatmeal cookie recipe! Actually, he needed the rifle and didn't really care about the cookie recipe, but he didn't want to break with tradition. The men have come to enjoy Andy's barter system."

"What about those boxes you left with Andy to take to the post office?"

"They're packed with clothes I'll never use up here. I'm sending them to my sister in Virginia."

Casey slid his hand around her neck and pulled her to him. "You tricked me. I thought you were leaving Alaska."

"Not me. I'm going to hang in here and try my luck at fishing."

He lay his hand on the inside of her thigh and drew lazy circles with his thumb. "I'm going to keep you happy. If you don't like fishing, I'll find other activities to keep you busy." His thumb inched higher up her leg.

'Mmmmmm," Alex purred. She knew she'd like those other activities.

"And no more talk about Bubba's breeding potential and Eskimo babies."

"But Bubba's breeding potential is important to me. Casey, I love the feeling of flying along behind a pack of huskies. I'm buying his four-dog racing team. And in the spring I get first pick of his lead dog's litter."

Casey looked at her sideways. "You mean you were actually oiling harnesses the other night?"

"What did you think we were doing?"

"I, uh, I thought maybe you were interested in Bubba's husband and fatherhood potential."

Alex smiled and snuggled into Casey. "I'm only interested in one man's husband and fatherhood potential. And I'm not interested in any exotic alternatives to creating a family."

"We're going to make babies the old-fashioned way," Casey said. "Will you marry me?"

"Will you promise to pick up after yourself?"

"No, but I'll hire a cleaning lady."

Alex stuck her hand out. "Deal."

"Deal," Casey murmured, pulling her close to him for a kiss that was achingly sweet and fiercely binding.

THE EDITOR'S CORNER

I am delighted to let you know that from now on one new LOVESWEPT each month will be simultaneously published in hardcover under the Doubleday imprint. The first LOVESWEPT in hardcover is **LONG TIME COMING**, by Sandra Brown, which you read—and we hope, loved—this month. Who better to start this new venture than the author of the very first LOVESWEPT, **HEAVEN'S PRICE**? We know that most of you like to keep your numbered paperback LOVESWEPTs in complete sets, but we thought many might also want to collect these beautifully bound hardcover editions. And, at only $12.95, a real bargain, they make fabulous gifts, not only at this holiday season but also for birthdays, Mother's Day, and other special occasions. Perhaps through these classy hardcover editions you will introduce some of your friends to the pleasures of reading LOVESWEPTs. When you ask your bookseller for the hardcover, please remember that the imprint is Doubleday.

Next month's simultaneously published hardcover and paperback is a very special treat from Fayrene Preston, the beginning of the trilogy *The Pearls of Sharah*. In these three LOVESWEPTs, a string of ancient, priceless pearls moves from person to person, exerting a profound effect on the life of each. The trilogy opens with **ALEXANDRA'S STORY**, LOVESWEPT #306 (no number, of course, on the hardcover edition). When Alexandra Sheldon turned to meet Damon Barand, she felt as if she'd waited her whole life for him. Damon—enigmatic, mysterious, an arms dealer operating just barely on the right side of the law—was the dark side of the moon beckoning Alex into the black satin night of his soul. But was it the woman he was drawn to? Or the impossibly beautiful and extravagantly valuable pearls she wore draped on her sensual body? This fascinating question answered, you'll be eager, we believe, for the two *Pearls of Sharah* romances to follow: in April, **RAINE'S STORY**; in June,

(continued)

LEAH'S STORY. You can count on the fact that all three books are breathlessly exciting reads!

Get ready for an offering from Judy Gill that's as poignant as it is playful, LOVESWEPT #307, **LIGHT ANOTHER CANDLE.** Sandy is rebuilding her life, at last doing the landscaping work she loves, when Richard Gearing comes bumping into her life. For Rick it is love at first sight; for Sandy it is torment from first encounter. Both had suffered terribly in their first marriages, and both are afraid of commitment. It takes her twin daughters, his young son, and a near tragedy to get these two gorgeous people together in one of the best surprise endings you'll ever hope to see in a love story.

Here comes one of the most original and thrilling romances we've published—**NEVER LET GO,** LOVESWEPT #308, by Deborah Smith. We're going to return to that super couple in **HOLD ON TIGHT,** Dinah and Rucker McClure. Their blissful life together has gone sadly awry—Dinah has disappeared and Rucker has been searching for her ceaselessly for almost a year. He finds her as the book opens, and it is a hellish reunion. Trust shattered, but still deeply in love with Dinah, Rucker is pulled into a dangerous, heart-wrenching chase for the woman he loves. Filled with passion and humor and surprises, this story of love regained is as unique as it is wonderful.

Please give a *big* welcome to a brand-new author, Lynne Marie Bryant, making her publishing debut with the utterly charming **CALYPSO'S COWBOY,** LOVESWEPT #309. When Smokejumper Caly Robbins parachuted onto the wilderness ranch, she expected to fight a fire—not to be swept into the arms of one thoroughly masculine, absolutely gorgeous black-haired cowboy. Jeff Adams was a goner the minute he set eyes on the red-haired, petite, and feisty lady. But her independence and his need to cherish and protect put them almost completely at odds . . . except when he was teaching her the sweet mysteries of love. A rich, vibrant love story from an author who writes authentically about ranchers 'cause she is one!

(continued)

Helen Mittermeyer follows up her thrilling **ABLAZE** with another hot romance next month, **BLUE FLAME**, LOVESWEPT #310, in which we get Dev Abrams's love story. Dev thinks he's hallucinating when he meets the shocked eyes of the only woman he has ever loved, the wife who supposedly died a few years before. Felicity, too, is stunned, for Dev had been reported killed in the middle of a revolution. But still burning brightly is the blue flame of their almost savage desire for each other, of their deep love. In a passionate and action-filled story, Dev and Felicity fight fiercely to reclaim their love. A must read!

Patt Bucheister gives us one of her best ever in **NEAR THE EDGE**, LOVESWEPT #311, the suspenseful tale of two people who were meant for each other. Alex Tanner had agreed to guard the daughter of a powerful man when fate made her the pawn in her brother's risky gambit. But the passion whipping between him and Joanna Kerr made it almost impossible for him to do his job. Set in Patt's native land, England, this is a very special novel, close to the author's heart . . . and, we suspect, one that will grow close to your heart, too.

Altogether a spectacular month ahead of great LOVE-SWEPT reading.

Warm good wishes,

Carolyn Nichols

Carolyn Nichols
 Editor
LOVESWEPT
Bantam Books
666 Fifth Avenue
New York, NY 10103

LOVESWEPT

Love Stories you'll never forget
by authors you'll always remember

☐	21863	**The Widow and the Wildcatter #246** Fran Barker	$2.50
☐	21887	**Silk On the Skin #247** Linda Cajio	$2.50
☐	21888	**The Object Of His Affection #248** Sara Orwig	$2.50
☐	21889	**January In July #249** Joan Elliott Pickart	$2.50
☐	21882	**Let's Do It Again #250** Janet Bieber	$2.50
☐	21890	**The Luck Of the Irish #251** Patt Bucheister	$2.50
☐	21891	**Adam's Fall #252** Sandra Brown	$2.50
☐	21900	**The Trouble with JJ #253** Tami Hoag	$2.50
☐	21893	**The Grand Finale #254** Janet Evanovich	$2.50
☐	21894	**Hold On Tight #255** Deborah Smith	$2.50
☐	21895	**Outlaw Derek #256** Kay Hooper	$2.50
☐	21896	**The Man From Half Moon Bay #257** Iris Johansen	$2.50
☐	21679	**Conflict Of Interest #258** Margia McDonnell	$2.50
☐	21902	**Warm Fuzzies #259** Joan Elliott Pickart	$2.50
☐	21903	**Divine Design #260** Mary Kay McComas	$2.50
☐	21904	**Baby, Baby #261** Barbara Boswell	$2.50
☐	21901	**For Love Of Lacey #262** Sandra Chastain	$2.50
☐	21906	**Hawk O'Toole's Hostage #263** Sandra Brown	$2.50
☐	21907	**The Brass Ring #264** Susan Crose	$2.50
☐	21908	**The Enchanting Miss Annabella #265** Joan Elliott Pickart	$2.50
☐	21909	**Flynn's Fate #266** Patt Bucheister	$2.50
☐	21910	**Made For Each Other #267** Doris Parmett	$2.50
☐	21911	**Strictly Business #268** Linda Cajio	$2.50
☐	21892	**Ablaze #269** Helen Mittermeyer	$2.50

Prices and availability subject to change without notice.

Buy them at your local bookstore or use this page to order:

- -

Bantam Books, Dept. SW3, 414 East Golf Road, Des Plaines, IL 60016

Please send me the books I have checked above. I am enclosing $_____
(please add $2.00 to cover postage and handling). Send check or money order
—no cash or C.O.D.s please.

Mr/Ms _____

Address _____

City/State _____ Zip _____

SW3—10/88

Please allow four to six weeks for delivery. This offer expires 4/89.